VIRTUAL LAW 1:
REUNIONS

Brandon Hill

Mythical Legends Publishing

A **Mythical Legends Publishing**
Mass-Market Paperback Edition

Copyright © 2015 by **Brandon Hill**
Published by **Mythical Legends Publishers**, 2017
Publisher@mythicallegends.com
http://mythicallegends.com

ISBN-10: **1943958-25-4**
ISBN-13: **978-1-943958-25-2**

Printed in the United States of America
9 8 7 6 5 4 3 2 1

DEDICATION

For my Aunt Donna, with love.
Thanks for always believing in me.

A Night at Pink's

"So how's the pot roast?" Jackie asked.

"Should be called 'rot roast.'"

"Hamburgers?"

"You really want me to make a pun of that?"

Jackie exhaled, long and loud, not bothering to hide her exasperation. She then put down the menu and glanced to her right and left furtively, scanning the restaurant's scant guest numbers, none human besides herself and Kate. "So, is there anything good, or did you just bring me here to gross me out?"

"Hey, I'm doing this for your last favor," Kate reminded her friend. "We could always stop."

"That's not what I meant." The tiny white beads at the ends of Jackie's cornrow braids rattled as she shook her head. "It's just that this place is on the Bridge, way out in the boonies, and you can't even tell me what's good?"

"Try the eggs," Kate said.

"Eggs?" Jackie's expression switched from incredulity to dismay. "That's it? Just the eggs?"

"They're good eggs."

Jackie stared at Kate's faint smile, grumbled something nigh inaudible, and then buried her face back into the menu.

"I guess you've been here before," she said after a

long moment of silence.

"Of course."

"Why do you like it here, then? I mean, it's on the Bridge!"

"What do you have against the Bridge?" Kate asked with a frown. "Don't tell me you're spooked by off-planers. That's not a healthy mindset to have in our line of work, you know."

"No, it's not that. It's just…" Jackie's voice faltered and began to trail off.

"You'd think that a person with your job would deal better with off-planers," Kate said. "Man's folly for screwing with the fabric of the universe. They're not just going to go away, you know."

"I told you, that's not it!" Jackie snapped. Taking care not to raise her voice, her whisper became a sharp hiss.

"I'm sure," Kate remarked blandly. "So what is it, then?"

"I'm just curious about why you like this place so much," Jackie said. The décor, a mix of green and white striped wallpaper bordering yellowing sheetrock, all held together by thin plywood panels and plascrete sealant seemed just as cobbled together as any of the structures on the Bridge, but in a curiously well-kept way. Though the table had more than a few graffiti and carvings on its surface, the tableware was clean, the menus were pristine, and there were rows of photographs neatly lined up in wooden frames on the yellowing sheet rock walls. "I mean, it's not much to look at, and the food sucks, so why bother?"

"History."

Jackie gave Kate a blank stare.

"The Yellow Snowmen, D-Stroy, and Cornucopia," Kate said, pointing towards the nearest row of photos, catty corner to their booth. "This place has been host to some of my favorite bands. I used to hang out here with Stacie and Tex before I joined the League, back when I was still working at Cybersoft. They'd have indie cover groups here every Saturday night; I loved 'em. Too bad the new management shut it down." She pointed towards a small stage on the restaurant's far side, obscured in darkness that had not seen light in years. Its curtains were dingy and laced with cobwebs, and the floorboards were buckling. "Guess he didn't think rockers attracted the demographic he wanted. He's suffering for it now; people sure as hell didn't come here for the food."

Jackie made a tiny cough. "Well, well, girlfriend, I didn't think you were a rock chick. For some reason, you don't strike me as that type."

"Oh?" Kate said, raising an eyebrow. "What *did* I strike you as?"

"You looked more like a classical music girl to me," Jackie said. "You know, Mozart and krid like that?"

"I like that as well," Kate admitted with a nod. "I'm just not picky with music. But I guess I'm a rocker at heart. Hell, I wanted to be a singer when I was a kid."

"A singer?" Jackie gave an amused grin. "Now *that* I can imagine."

"Really?" Kate said.

"You got the look down pat."

Kate laughed as she watched Jackie's eyes scan her clothing, a blue cotton blouse over old black jeans. These looked more like thrift store duds than any of the hyper-stylish to gaudy apparel of the stars that were on the tank. Her looks were exotic, attributing to the Asian heritage on her mother's side, but only modestly so, surely not camera material. Her nose was too close to her lips, and her eyes appeared too big for her face.

Then Jackie gestured towards a photo of a band on the opposite wall. One of the trio was a tall, muscular black man with a keyboard slung across his back; the second, the bassist, was an off-planer with gold skin and a crown of horns that grew from his scalp; the third was a woman in black denim jeans and jacket that she left unzipped to reveal a leather bustier, also black. She had a guitar proudly in her arms. Her dark hair was cropped and styled into wisps with soft purple highlights, so different from Kate's thick, bodiless ebony mop. There was a mischievous light in her eyes as she half-smiled.

"You look like her, as a matter of fact," Jackie said, glancing at the picture and then back towards Kate. "Come to think of it, you look a lot like her."

Kate twisted around to view the picture more closely. "You think so?" She said. "Well, color me flattered."

Jackie nodded. "Um, who is she, by the way?"

"No freakin' way!" Kate twisted back around and slammed her hands on the tabletop, startling a few of the nearby restaurant guests. "I *had* to have told you about Ambush!"

"I… gather you like 'em?" Jackie said, taken aback by Kate's unexpected gush.

"You better believe it. I used to come here whenever they had a concert. I'd sneak out of the house and get in on my looks … if you know what I mean."

Jackie licked her dry lips, her face froze into an ambivalent grimace.

"You used to whore yourself out to see a rock group?" It sounded more like a statement than a question.

"Yeah," Kate said. "I was with the band… *all* of them."

Kate noticed that Jackie's normally chocolate colored skin had actually turned pale.

Kate sat silent and straight-faced for a moment more, inviting Jackie to almost buy into her statement. At last, a half-smile broke out on her face. It broadened; she squeezed her eyes shut, and shook in barely-contained laughter.

"Aw!" Jackie feigned throwing a silverware roll, and then snorted. "Well then, it looks like you saved me from giving you too much credit."

"You mean you're actually disappointed that I didn't whore myself out for a concert?" Kate asked.

"Forget it," Jackie said, waving dismissively. "But still, you *do* look like that chick in the photo."

"Chevroness."

"Who?"

"That's her name," Kate said, gesturing casually

towards the painting. "Her stage name, at least. But you're right; I *do* kinda look like her. I'm surprised I never noticed it before."

"You two could be related, to tell the truth," Jackie said, giving the picture a more studious stare. "Her hair's shorter, not quite as thick, and her nose is longer, but out, rather than down. That's about it."

A strange look came over Kate's face. It was brief and vague, almost like a grimace. It passed, but not before Jackie noticed it. "Something wrong?" She said.

"It's nothing." Kate shook her head. "Just a thought."

"Penny for it," Jackie said.

"I said it's nothing," Kate said, more forcefully.

"Okay, okay," Jackie said, raising her hands in a warding gesture. "Geez, don't bite my head off." She checked her watch. "You know, we ought to order. You gotta be at work soon, right?"

"Not for another hour," Kate said, removing her credplate from her wallet. She placed it into the slot on the wall beside the table and made her choice from the selections that appeared on the touch screen above it. "Besides, we're on the Bridge." She pointed to the windows by the restaurant's entrance. Beyond the Bridge's stainless steel girders, the League Pyramid loomed above the harbor and the skyline. "HQ's just a straight shot down the highway."

"Yeah, but it takes a good fifteen minutes for you to get your uniform on, let alone sync with all the nano-crap in it, right?" Jackie mulled over her own meal decision for a moment longer, and then sulked while she finally punched in her choice.

"Geez, what'd you order?" Kate said in a sympathetic tone. "The look on your face was like you went and asked for the chili."

Again, Jackie blanched. "Oh, God… I *did* ask for the chili."

"Toilet paper's a blessing and a curse," Kate said, pursing her lips, "and you'll be finding that out before the day's done."

"That bad, huh?" Jackie said.

"Well, I did tell you to stick with the eggs," Kate answered. "But then again, you probably don't have that much to worry about. I mean, when they hook you up to your console, don't you have a catch tube installed in your…?"

"It can overload if I'm sick," Jackie said.

"I doubt you'll get *that* sick," Kate replied. "I've seen you eat stuff a vacuum cleaner won't. Not to mention I'm one of the few people who's actually seen you eat. Most of the folks back at HQ think you spend your life hooked up to the mainframe's systems, with the computers just socking the food to your veins."

"Is that a fact?" Jackie said.

"You sound surprised."

"Well, it ain't all that shocking, come to think of it," Jackie mused aloud. "After all, I do run some long hours there. And I gotta admit, being on the I-Link is a helluva lot more exciting than the real world."

"I resent that," Kate said. "The real world's my jurisdiction after all. Well, mostly."

"And there are folks at HQ who think that you enforcers don't ever take your uniforms off," Jackie remarked with a broad grin, "but I know better."

"Well, it's easier to leave it on," Kate said. When she nodded, it seemed sad, almost grave. "But I don't. I think the others are crazy to do it."

"Why's that?" Jackie said. "The stuff I've seen you do with it over the security cams-"

"So now you're a voyeur?" Kate said, eyeing Jackie curiously.

"Hey! That's not what I meant," Jackie snapped.

"I know." Kate made a soft laugh. "You kinda left yourself wide open for that one."

"Well, I meant it," Jackie said. "The krid you can do with that suit sometimes makes me want to become an enforcer myself."

"You like what you do too much," Kate said, shaking her head. "'Sides, it's not as easy as it looks."

"What could be so tough about it, besides the training?" Jackie asked.

Again, Kate fixed her with an odd gaze, but covered just as quickly as before.

"If you only knew," she said.

"Knew what?"

"Training's the easy part," Kate replied. "But the synching … That's something else entirely. I've seen men, bigger and stronger than me, lose their minds."

She stared at her open, empty right hand. Beads

of condensation still clung to her skin from the glass of iced tea she had been nursing from when they first arrived. She flexed her fingers once, as if testing to see if they were real. "It's like having to learn how to control new limbs, like having an infinite supply of arms and legs. They load your nervous system up with so many bionics just to make it a part of yourself, you begin to wonder if your every move will start going with a sound effect. Some people ... they didn't take well to the synching. It unbalanced them mentally for a time; some ... they just ..."

Her voice trailed off.

Jackie was silent.

"Just be glad you didn't have to go through that," Kate said. "At least all your implants were voluntary. And most of the stuff you do in the I-Link is automatic." She glanced at Jackie, again with her curious stare. "So, you still want to join the family?"

"Well... you gave me a lot to think about; that's for sure," Jackie said. She gave a nervous laugh.

"Getting cold feet now, Jacks?" Kate said. "That's not like you."

Jackie shook her head resolutely. "No, not really. It's just a bit more than I thought, is all."

"You know, having a suit that becomes an extension of you isn't the only plus about being an enforcer," Kate said.

"It isn't?"

Discreetly, Kate's hand went to the CANCEL icon on the ordering screen.

"Another thing is the obscene amount of tech we're hooked up to, like detection software," Kate said. "It's designed to search for just about anything, you know. Hidden people, places, things, I-Link anomalies, illegal gateways…" Her metallic gray eyes locked dead onto Jackie's large brown ones. "Brain riders …"

Kate had barely finished the last word when Jackie sprang from her seat. But Kate reacted with near-invisible speed. In a fraction of a second, Jackie was slammed back against her seat, held securely by the neck against the wall by a pair of black tendrils. The projections grew from the sleeve of Kate's blouse –now distended and sheathing her hand and forearm in black–, wrapped double around Jackie's neck and impaled into the booth's wall, at first soft and malleable as leather, and then solid as steel.

"Don't make a scene," Kate said. "You'll scare the civvies, and I'll have to inject you with some of my own nanos. You know the rest, I think: You'll go night-night with Jackie, stuck in that body, and then the League techies will have to pry you out. That means tracing you, and going through all the legal krid that I hate. Worst part is you'll be executed for hacking a League operative. So why don't you just come on out of there and save me a lot of boring paperwork?"

"Not if I kill her first." "Jackie" made a sneering, smart aleck grin. "I could stop her heart if I wanted."

"Don't flatter yourself," Kate said. "We both know you won't do it. And even if you did, don't think that I'd stop you. Jackie made a commitment to the League,

16

the same as me. She knew what that would mean, just as well as I do."

"You don't have the…"

She froze in mid-sentence. Her eyes went wide, and then rolled up into her head. A small trickle of blood ran down her neck from the enfolding layers of tendrils.

"You were saying something?" Kate said. "Kinda uncomfortable for you, isn't it? I can make the arm's edge sharper if you like, but then I think you'd be suffering from a bad case of 'look, ma, no head' syndrome."

Kate waited a second more to make her point, then dulled the edges. She watched as "Jackie" relaxed with relief, and chose to speak again.

"Well, it looks like you got it all figured out, huh?" The quality of the rider's voice had changed into something completely unlike the Jackie that Kate knew. It was hollow, more direct, and mocking. There was now no question as to the type of presence that managed to subsume her friend.

"Now I know what you are," Kate said. "Scared kridless one moment, talking krid the next; you sure act like a hacker; I thought you'd be a bigger fish."

"You're perceptive. How'd you guess it so fast?"

"Like you said, I'm perceptive." Kate said with a shrug. "Jackie knows that I don't take the suit off until my days off. She's not that much into small talk; she likes to keep it down to important stuff. Also, she knows more about my past than I do, and never lets me forget it. She also hates it when I call her 'Jacks.' Oh yeah, and when I told her about Ambush, she knows that I don't gush like some airhead teeny-bopper."

"Wow, man, it sure looks like I screwed up," the hacker said, still eerily confident. "Not that it matters. I didn't get much from you, but it was enough."

"Data mining?" Kate said. "You could've just tapped the source. What happened? League mainframe was too much for you? No chance of you telling me what company you work for, I guess."

"I'm not working for a company," the hacker answered. "And here's another surprise: I'm not exactly what you'd really call a 'hacker.'"

"So what are you, then?" Kate said, feeling her patience beginning to slip. This … whatever she was, was definitely fond of talking, but was telling her nothing. And despite being in direct contact, her own scans gave her another big goose egg, save presence of a rider.

"I alone am not your worry," the presence said. "But my colleagues have a great interest in the League … specifically its defenses. You were my primary target, as a matter of fact. But we underestimated the software in your suit's man-machine interface. You've got some really badass krid on you. But your friend was a bit too easy to get into. So I just used her to get what I needed from you."

"I didn't give you anything sensitive," Kate said. "Any monkey can get the stuff I said off the I-Link."

"General stuff," the presence said, "not specifics, which you *did* give me. Like just how hard it is to sync with your nanos. That ring a bell?"

"One whole thing," Kate said dryly.

"Small steps, is what I call it," the presence replied. There was no arrogance in the voice, no swagger, but plenty of salt. "Not to mention the fact that we *did* find a weakness in the League's defenses. Good ol' flawed humans. What d'you say to that?"

"Give us time," Kate said, and smiled. "You know you can't sting us in the same place twice."

"Maybe we don't want to," the presence said. "Maybe we'll just rest satisfied that the League isn't perfect."

"What've you got against the League anyway?" Kate said, more curious than frustrated. "They're the reason why humans still exist on this planet anyway, and why all of creation wasn't just turned into millions of kingdoms for God knows what. Are you even faintly aware of the dangers of screwing around with dimensions?"

The presence laughed –not mocking, only amused.

"Typical of League dogs: bred to think we're all stupid … that we couldn't possibly know, that we couldn't ever fully appreciate what it is you do. Some of us remember the war just fine. How can we not, when the League never lets us forget it? And of course, you blow things out of proportion, in your favor. If it's one thing you do well, it's keep the propaganda wheels turning."

Kate was silent. Against her better judgment, she tasted the words the brain-rider and realized that in the back of her mind, even though they were the banter of a common thug, they made a sort of perverse sense. She'd seen enough of the world as a member of Cybersoft, and enough of the other worlds as an enforcer to be less than pleased with the League's handling of the technology and planet they'd inherited after the war.

"Your eyes are opening," the presence said. Jackie's face made a knowing grin. Kate replied with a sour look.

"Good; you didn't insult my intelligence by denying it," the presence said. "That means you're smarter than most."

"Am I really, now?" Kate said flatly. "Maybe I just called for backup."

"Maybe you did, but I won't be around for that long."

"I firewalled Jackie's bionics when my blades cut you," Kate said. "You're not going anywhere."

Again, the presence laughed. "Ever arrogant, eh? You League types really are all cut from the same mold. We're not without our own resources, and some of us are just damn good." Jackie's body sighed. "But now you're starting to bore me. And this body's getting a crick in its neck, so I'll be going now."

"Excuse me?" Kate said, half in disbelief. Was this brain-rider stupid or was he or she really that good? League firewalls were supposed to be impossible to break. "Yes, enforcer chick," the presence said with a wink. "I am just that good… better than you, even. Oh, and just to prove it…"

A surge of electricity cut through Kate's forearm: a

spear of pure pain tearing through her fingertips, down through the knuckles, wrists and into her elbow. Her muscles hardened reflexively as she yelped and pulled it back, the force of the shock knocking her against the back of the seat. The tendrils from her uniform buckled and went limp, unfastening themselves from Jackie's neck.

Kate watched as Jackie's eyes un-focused, crossed, then shut. She slumped down, and fell limply into the booth.

Groaning, Kate righted herself. With residual pain shooting though her arm, she grasped her wrist and swore. Her vision refocused and she squeezed the remaining tears from her eyes. She looked across the restaurant, and was relieved to find that no one had noticed what had gone on. Jackie, however, had collapsed sideways in the booth. Shaking off and then ignoring the lingering pain and numbness in her arm, she hopped out of her seat and went to her friend's side. Seeing the small gash in her neck, she took several napkins from the holder, and pressed them against the wound. She tried to use her suit to inject her with repair nanobots, but the shock had overloaded the man-machine interface. Her biocomp informed her that it was still trying to compensate. Even the tendrils from her suit hadn't retracted. They hung flaccidly from her fingertips, slowly sagging across the surface of the table and seat like caramelized ink.

"Jackie, speak to me!" Kate said, tapping her on the right cheek. "You still in there?"

Jackie's eyes fluttered, and then went wide as they focused on her.

"You remember who I am?" Kate said.

"'Course I do," Jackie said, sounding almost offended. "You're the grand duchess of Gaia, come for tea."

Kate grimaced, but was surprised at how it seemed that nothing had happened. "It's you all right. But I think that rider made your sense of humor even lamer."

"You know, if my head didn't feel like it had a baby, I'd hit you," Jackie said.

"My point."

Jackie sat up and winced. She took the napkins from Kate and pressed them hard against her neck. "Gawd, what'd you do, girl? Try to cut my head off or something?"

"You had a brain-rider in you," Kate said. "How much do you remember?"

"Bits and pieces. I think it happened yesterday, back at work, when I was still hooked up to the mainframe. He must've been waiting for me in the system, probably trapped by the security subroutines, so he couldn't get out the same way he came in. How he hacked so deep, though, that's something I'd like to know." She glanced around. "So we came here to eat?"

"Not anymore," Kate said, helping Jackie to her feet. "You can walk? It's almost time to be at work."

"You're kidding!" Jackie said in dismay as her stomach made an audible growl.

"Don't get that way with me," Kate answered as

her biocomp finished rebooting, and her uniform reset itself, again becoming indistinguishable from everyday fabric. Hurriedly, she made a scan for the brain-rider, and then relaxed. Jackie was clean. "I just saved your cyberized ass… not to mention my pride. 'Sides, you're probably in for a little time at the infirmary, probably a CAT scan too. I'm pretty sure you're clean, but I won't be completely satisfied until I make sure that rider didn't leave anything behind."

Jackie's stomach growled again as she righted herself. Supported by Kate on her right side, they began to make their way to the exit. "Aw, man! And I gotta eat the food at the HQ cafeteria!"

"Trust me," Kate said. "It's a step up from this place."

"Then why'd you come here?" Jackie said.

"Never mind. We had this conversation before."

###

24

25

Reunions

He looked like a Rastafarian ninja. That was Alicia's first impression of Bob's new avatar. The last time, he looked like a commando smurf; the time before that, a Buddha with the head of a guppy; the madness went on. But his penchant for odd avatar constructs was how she came to recognize him. If it wasn't weird, it wasn't Bob. She'd long since become used to it. Tolerance for eccentricity was a small price to pay for his skills. God knew she needed the money, and pulling jobs through Bob was better than hooking up with loan sharks. Royalties from her dwindling album sales still kept food in her mouth, but with the breakup of the band and no new songs released in over five years, it was the money from her jobs that kept Alicia's soul alive. And doses of circus weren't getting any cheaper.

"Jah love, girl! Big things a'guan pon de worlds!" Alicia had to admit that he'd affected an admittedly decent Jamaican patois for his greeting.

"Hey, Bob. Still perfectly normal as ever, I see?"

Bob smiled, and switched back to his normal manner of speech. "Not if I can help it, baby. Got the newest krid for you, though. Interested?"

Alicia liked Bob. With money, he was always right to business. "Fire away," she said.

"Well, it's actually one thing," Bob's avatar, with its limited range of facial expressions made a sort of blur between a smile and a frown. "Seems the guy who gave me this is an old friend of yours."

"Really?" The tone of her voice had shifted to that of both piqued interest and wariness.

"Before you say anything," the avatar held up its hands innocently, "you know security on my end's airtight; always has been. I even ran a background check on the guy. He's not an enforcer or I-Link cop; that I know. 'Matter of fact, if I hadn't found out one particular thing, I wouldn't have bothered with him."

"Well, stuff the excuses and spit it out," Alicia said.

"All right, then. Does the name, 'Walker,' ring a bell?"

Alicia raised an eyebrow. "Say what, now?"

"Yeah, yeah, he's supposed to be dead," Bob said. "Hell, several worlds other than Earth know he's dead, but honey ... it's gotta be him."

"What makes you so sure?" Alicia said. Bob had sick hacking skills that made her look like a third-rate noob, but even they couldn't change the facts of the universe. There was no mistake. It had been all over the news. She'd personally identified Walker's remains and attended his funeral.

An e-mail notification flashed against her field of vision. Alicia answered it.

Don't hate me, sunflower, was the text part of the message, followed by a video feed. The image came in crystal clear and instantly recognizable. It was the inside of his apartment –namely the bedroom, the date on the lower right hand side from five years ago. The sounds from the audio feed made the origins of the clip unmistakable: those of the two figures upon the bed caught in an intimate moment –and one was definitely him. The other was herself.

Curiosity became anger as Alicia switched off the video feed.

"Where did you get this?" Alicia struggled to keep her voice level despite her emotions.

"He sent it to me," Bob said. "Told me to give it to you."

"Don't you lie to me, Bob!" Alicia barked at the avatar, whose edges pixilated as she swiped her hand through the hologram. "Whose sick idea of a joke was this? Dammit, he told me…!"

"…Told you that he destroyed the only copy, that you and him got back at the hacker who broke into your OnBoard, stole the original and tried to blackmail you. You rewrote the security programs on his own OnBoard, and replaced them with Mind Flayer ice, putting the rat bastard in Ragnarok, with one eighth of his brain fried. Then you destroyed the copy before it could wind up on the I-Link, and gave the original to him."

Alicia went numb. "Good God, Bob…" She felt her body slump back into the sofa as her anger was thoroughly extinguished, and replaced by an eerie sense of wonder. "Only Walker knew that."

"If it ain't Walker, then he's channeling his restless soul," Bob said. "This guy even remembered that time we met in the middle of the Mojave right before the run on Gaea's Atrepasi mainframe. That was in a dead zone, girl: no phones, no GPS, no I-Link. No one else could have known about it!"

Walker. The name brought back a flood of memories: small points of light in her dark past. She never knew his full name when she was holed up in that compound with the other kids the sifters had scooped off of the streets for the underground sweatshops and brothels, but he was the first who talked to her. His defiance inspired her to keep her sanity and at last escape along with two other musically-inclined inmates: a keyboardist named T.J. and Rax, an off-planer who could work magic with drums. On the outside, Walker's hacking skills got her and their struggling rock band, Ambush, the funds to become the sensation remembered by millions. She and Walker were lovers for a time, but their livelihoods ultimately took them apart from each other. She was devastated when he died, his charred body found on the back streets behind New York's old transcon bridge after a large explosion; even worse was the authorities had no idea how it had happened.

It was this, along with the arrest of Rax on charges of aiding and abetting known hackers and dimensional pirates, and the shock of his subsequent death in prison by a shiv to his vital third heart over a pack of cigarettes, that began a downward spiral into her current situation, with her jobs under Bob and daily doses of circus as all that remained of her once glamorous life.

It was impossible for Alicia to hold back the flood of

emotions as she considered the almost inconceivable, ludicrous possibility that despite what she'd been forced to see in the morgue, and despite logic altogether, perhaps Walker might -just might- not be dead after all.

But if this was all a ploy, who could be after her? She'd covered her backside well enough in those bygone days, and even now, especially with Bob watching over her. Krid, the e-mail even had the pet name Walker had given her. No one else but him knew it.

But Bob had never lied to her before.

"Are you absolutely sure it was him?" She said. It was a question and a warning.

"I'm positive." Bob said it straightforwardly and without any trace of doubt.

"What did he want?"

Her ONboard made a shrill chirp, and the words, UPLOAD COMPLETE shone superimposed upon her field of vision.

"Everything he gave me is in the files I just sent you," Bob said. "And just so you know, I robbed him blind for this little service. Thing is, he didn't seem to care."

"Money was never an object for him, that's for sure," Alicia said wistfully, more to herself than anyone else.

"Careful there," Bob said slyly. His avatar made a half-lidded, cartoonishly large grin. "You'll make your girlfriend jealous."

"Kumai isn't my girlfriend," Alicia said, more vehemently than she'd wanted.

"Coulda fooled me," Bob said, on the edge of

laughter. "You left the telepresence unit on last night, you know."

"And you spied on us?" Alicia was completely livid. This, however, was quickly replaced with embarrassment. It was that same little mistake that had led to Bob's copy of the video feed that might have ruined her career. It wouldn't have been a big deal this time around; the paparazzi had long since stopped hounding her, but even now she tended to keep up a fair level of discretion. Last night, the first time in awhile that Kumai had gone farther than allowing Alicia to sleep in her lap, was the absolute worst time to have dropped the ball. Her saving grace was that it was only Bob who had seen them.

The avatar waved its arms emphatically. "No, no! I was only gonna leave you a message about Walker last night. I saw the viewer was on; I thought you were online. I couldn't help seeing what I saw; I'm no voyeur, girl. Off-planers don't do krid for me anyway, Gaeans especially."

"I swear, Bob, you tell anyone …"

"Hey, you know I've got more class than that," Bob sounded almost hurt. "Anyways, just remember to pay me this time."

"Just as long as you give me what's mine," Alicia said, and forwarded the money to his account.

"Enjoy your reunion, baby."

He vanished as she gave him the finger.

***

Alicia supposed that Kumai believed she hadn't slept in hours; the truth was, she hadn't. Her bodiless shoulder-length black hair was frazzled, her thrift store black jeans and white tank top looked as if they had been picked out of an unfolded pile, and there were bags under her pale eyes that could have classified as luggage carry-ons as she rattled off the news to her off-planer roommate, talking as if someone had filled her veins with pure sugar. Kumai, a polar opposite to Alicia, with her immaculate eggshell business robes and luxurious falls of crystal white hair, sipped placidly at her cup of jeeva all the while. She appeared to be listening, but with her liquid black eyes it was hard to tell.

"...And so Walker wants me to do this dramatic jailbreak thing, out of Ragnarok, of all places!" Alicia continued, her words running together so quickly, her story read like a whole sentence. "He sent me everything I'd need: schematics, programs, codes, kitchen sink... everything I'd need to hit the mainframe. I was thinking he'd lost it at first, but when I saw all the krid he got me, I thought, 'Man, he's frickin' serious!' I mean, at first I thought Bob was jerking me, but after I saw all this, I thought, no way, man; this has gotta be Walker! No one would do something this suicidal! It's just... beautiful!"

"One might say that your I-Link games are suicidal as well," Kumai said, her high, soft voice, lilting, betraying a hint of concern in her placid exterior. She tilted her head to the side, resting her jeeva cup on its saucer. "As a matter of fact, Kumai thinks that they are most every time."

"Yeah, but this is Walker we're talking about, blueberry!" Alicia said, ranting on. "He's done stuff that'd turn you white as your hair! When he busted me and those kids outta that compound, he went back and broke into the Renfros' mainframe and turned every dirty secret of that place over to the feds. Took the bastards years to clean up from the kridstorm. And he almost single-handedly took out the Atrepasi after they screwed him over. Biggest organized crime syndicate in the worlds, and they were nothing to him! He was like the online Superman, or something!"

"What did Kumai tell you about taking circus in the morning?" Kumai said. Her eyebrows knotted and she shook her head slowly, this time giving no mystery to her feelings. "You know it makes you hyperactive."

"Hyper-nothing," Alicia said, although Kumai had been right. She couldn't wait to get started on the mission, and in her excitement, had jumped the gun on her next circus dosage. Though technically a hallucinogen, it also had stimulant qualities that made the DT's look like narcolepsy.

"Kumai worries about you, tir-Alicia," Kumai always used the pet name whenever she was most concerned.

"Kumai worries too damn much," Alicia said with a grimace. "Besides, Walker's the A-1 best. Nobody's better, period. If the League's I-Link cops have something that can stop him, then we'll deserve to get brain-fried."

She laid her fingers upon the top of Kumai's hand, suddenly much calmer, as if the worst of the circus had worn off. "By the way, Kumai, I've been meaning to ask you… once this job's over, I've been thinking about taking another whack at getting the band back together. I got a good feeling about this time, too. And if things work out, how about I make you my new manager?

"Kumai… is not sure." Her voice was distant and small. "Kumai is comfortable here."

"But with you being a business girl and all, this job would be the perfect fit," Alicia said. She never gave up easily when faced with the Gaean's evasiveness. "Give it some thought for me, please?" She fixed Kumai with the sad puppy-eyed look. It was not so much effective in getting what she wanted, but it did bring a cute reddish hue to Kumai's blue skin that made her laugh. And her own laugh made Kumai laugh. In the end, she half-heartedly conceded.

***

When the circus eventually wore off, Alicia slept for most of the day. Kumai was gone when she woke.

Kumai owned an apartment of her own on Gaea, but hung around Alicia so much that her place became like a second home. Alicia's income paid for Kumai's gateway passes, and so she had racked up an insane amount of frequent transfer points over the months they had known each other. Alicia never pried much into her private affairs; their relationship, born in a bar at the bottom level of Gaea's capital of Mezedia, came about through a lonely desire for company rather than personal interests, combined with the weird natural tendency of the Gaean third gender to "cling" to people they liked ... or so she supposed. This was why despite the fact that Alicia was generally a lone wolf, and knew next to nothing of Kumai's personal life, they got along strangely well. Gaeans, more specifically, the first two-thirds of their race, were an aloof lot, but Kumai, like the others of her sex, female in immediate appearance, but not in anatomy, was much more flexible in her demeanor and affection. She dressed as fancily as any of her kind, as if they all had a terminal case of expensive tastes, but her heart was far more "human."

Kumai really was a worrywart, though, Alicia thought, pursing her lips with annoyance at the off-planer's absence. Circus wasn't a problem. It sharpened her skills online, kept her edge. She had used it for years, since her glory days in Ambush. Nowadays, she only used it on runs, overindulging every now and again. But she had it all together; everything was under control.

She slipped out of bed, not bothering to get dressed, brought her OnBoard down to the living room, and pressed the power stud on the little black rectangle, just larger than a paperback novel. She threw herself into the couch across from the coffee table and sent a mental command from her INplant, configuring the OnBoard for direct access. She then extended the jack from its spool at her right temple. Its nanofibers found the port on the OnBoard and pulled it in with a tiny click.

She removed the circus from its container: a vial less than an inch in length and the thickness of a 2-D printer's ink cartridge, both for its potency and ease for smuggling inside ballpoint pen casings. They were airtight as to evade chemical sniffers in the mail: so much fuss for so little effort spent on controlling the trade. The League tended to not get involved in petty things like illegal drug trafficking like the law enforcement in the overburdened system of the old U.S. did before the World War III collapse; with their eyes set on profit, it mattered little what came across dimensional barriers as long as it was nothing that posed an immediate threat to Earth, and that the client could pay the transfer fees. Circus, therefore, was something left to the New York Megalopolis local authorities, who were notably less than adept at controlling it. It was kind of pathetic, really, the fact that independent law enforcement in the Giant Apple was practically helpless without the aid of the corporation that had lorded over all since the war.

"Hit me, baby," she said, and broke the vial into her eyes.

An instant before it happened, she wondered what was better at giving her the kind of pleasure that kept her going, Kumai, or the circus. The bliss of the latter, however, washed her mind free of those thoughts as the OnBoard accepted her password and shunted her into the I-Link. Combined pain and pleasure lashed her nervous system, and it began.

***

Two hours later, she awoke to Kumai wiping the blood from her nose and the side of her eyes. Her OnBoard was belching out black smoke, and a mini defibulater was adhered to her chest.

Alicia blinked once, and then coughed. "Holy krid, blueberry! Do I have a story to tell you!" She whispered.

"Tir-Alicia!" Kumai folded her into a near-choking embrace. "Kumai thought you were dead, but was too afraid to call an ambulance!"

"Nah, just taking a nap," Alicia said. She took the towel from the still-terrified Gaean, and finished wiping. "God, I still feel wasted!"

"Kumai wants you to stop using circus," the Gaean pleaded. "It is so, so bad for you, tir-Alicia!"

"And Alicia wants you to stop referring to yourself in the third person." She was becoming ever more annoyed with Kumai's constant concern about a problem that wasn't there. Nevertheless, she did seem pretty stressed about the whole ordeal. Despite the Gaean's obvious worry, she grinned wickedly and pinched Kumai's right cheek, gently stretching the tiny tear-shaped mole below her left eye in a strange way. Kumai winced.

"You're so cute when you're scared," she said with a naughty grin. "You know that?"

"You pick strange times to tell Kumai such things,"

Kumai said, rubbing her abused cheek after Alicia had let go. Alicia laughed. With their blue skin, seeing a Gaean blush was a funny sight.

"We're gonna have guests, blueberry," she said. "A communion with the dead, you might say."

"So Walker really is alive?"

"Alive and kicking," Alicia said, tapping the coffee table with her foot. "Oh yeah, rumors of his death have been greatly exaggerated. And now that this job's done, we've got some big plans, he and I. He's got some formalities to take care of, but after that, we're getting the band back together!"

Alicia broke into a peal of carefree, raucous laughter, tossing the soiled towel into the air. "This calls for a celebration!"

Kumai grabbed her arm while it was still raised; the towel fell limply to the ground. "No, tir-Alicia; no more circus!" A pool of tears started to form at the edges of her onyx eyes. "Please, do this for Kumai!"

"Oh, all right," Alicia said, deflated. "No circus, then, okay?"

"Kumai is satisfied." And though she showed no true look of satisfaction, Kumai released her grip.

"Well, then, now that that's settled," Alicia said, massaging her wrist, "we need to make some plans. Rax'll need some time to lay low."

"You told Kumai that Rax was dead."

Alicia made a guffaw. "Yeah, you heard that too, huh? Seems like we got people coming back from the dead right and left; you'd think God's on vacation, or something."

"Walker told you that he was not dead? That is who you tried to break out of jail?"

"'Tried,' nothing!" Alicia drawled. "What do you think I was doing on the I-Link for so long? My laundry? Walker showed him to me while riding a security node. Dunno what he was doing rotting out in Ragnarok; bastards in the League told me he was killed in a prison riot in Obsidian. Walker didn't find the whole truth, but he did say that Rax was meant to be the fall guy for the riots. They tucked him away nice and neat… or so they thought. We got him out, but there's no way in hell I'm letting the League corrections pukes get away with what they did to him."

"So what will you do?" Kumai said.

"Right now," Alicia made a very audible yawn, "I'm gonna go take a nap. "I'll need Bob's help for the next phase."

"Kumai is sleepy as well." Kumai made a long, deep yawn of her own, reclining on the side of her couch and kicking off her shoes, which were as white as her robes. Without another word, she retired to the bedroom, with Alicia watching her leave, feeling a twinge of annoyance at the Gaean's passive-aggressive ways. Kumai was usually her pillow when she chose to stay the night, but it looked as though tonight, her only pillows –soft as they were, would be the old, worn cloth ones on the couch, with the music files from her OnBoard as her only companion.

***

Ambush broke up soon after Rax was arrested. After the news of his death, Alicia lost hope for salvaging the band in any meaningful way. As far as she was concerned, if there was no Rax, there was no Ambush. Aside from I-Link runs for Bob's varied illicit businesses, her life took on a rhythm of eating, sleeping, and spending her evenings with Kumai. She hardly ever left home; Kumai was only there at night.

Tonight, Kumai was especially busy, holed up in the Tisvard food corporation's financial offices in Gaea doing paperwork. Tonight would be especially lonely, but the upside was that it gave Alicia time to repair her OnBoard and get what she needed from Bob.

The problem was that Bob wasn't answering her calls.

This never happened.

"Krid! Where the hell are you, man?" Alicia shouted into his voicemail after her fifth attempt. She fumed, wanting –and yet thankful that common sense prevented her– to throw the OnBoard to the ground. "He's never not there," she thought aloud. He was a bigger recluse than she was, doing all his business on the I-Link.

About an hour later, she realized that something was indeed, seriously wrong.

Two hours later, the abrupt e-mail confirmed it.

Bob is dead

Alicia was too numb to react at first. Perhaps this was why the line of code that loaded itself onto her OnBoard changed her state of mind so quickly. She scanned the contents of the new file. In a moment, the name, VIPER.EXE shone in her field of vision.

Alicia's initial confusion gave over to a deep, seething anger. She and Bob had worked closely over the years through the I-Link to the point where he'd become just as much a friend as he was a business colleague. It seemed so unreal that he was dead.

But why did he send a Viper program? Alicia wondered. Vipers were a rare and lethal virus type, and one of the few that evaded nearly all attempts to purge, except through special backdoor codebreakers that only experts could install.

In a moment, however, she figured out the reason for it, and anger and grief gave way to determination. Bob had trusted her the most out of all his contacts, and had probably planned the message to be sent in the event of an untimely death. And the message was simple. He wanted revenge.

But revenge against whom? She wondered. Was it the League? No, it couldn't be them. Bob was too small-time to be worth-

The phone rang, making her start. After an obligatory expletive, Alicia sent the command, and the tank in the center of the den came on with a faint static hum.

"Walker!" Alicia propped herself on her hands and knees at the couch's edge. Partially obscuring the soft features of the man in the hologram was a flip of hair darker than her own, and dyed with a stripe of white. He'd added more tribal tattoos to his face and had several more earrings in his ears since the days before his alleged death. Though they hadn't been an item in years, she could not help the blush that came to her cheeks. His green eyes still held that charming mischievous twinkle, so similar to her own.

"I'm taking a big risk calling you, sunflower, so listen up." Walker moved the fall of his hair away from his right eye as he spoke. "It might be awhile before we can talk again."

"Fire away, honey," Alicia said, tossing aside the wiry tangle of repair equipment from her OnBoard as she stood. "I'm all ears."

***

As amazed by Walker's explanation as she was, Alicia didn't like it. She asked him how he'd gotten the info, which consisted of very personal things that sometimes involved Kumai. Walker admitted he'd been keeping an eye on her for quite some time, but remained mum on exactly how he did it. Still, none of anything he had was surprising. She could try sweeping her apartment for bugs, but she knew that she wouldn't find any; it wasn't his style.

It was the League who'd had Bob iced, she learned. Odd as it seemed, it confirmed her first suspicion. This was a hacker's quintessential worst-case scenario, and

Walker admitted that he'd goofed. He ought to have contacted her himself, and not have gone through a middle man, but there had been too much at stake. Nevertheless, despite all his precautions, someone had outsmarted him. He'd been out of practice and allowed some League sifter in their I-Link police corps to tag him. They had become aware of most of his connections but not her, not yet. He'd made sure of that, once he became aware of the tag and fixed his OnBoard to remove it, but for Bob, it was too late. Enforcers had him tracked down and terminated before he could send warning. He and Rax were in a safe place for now, an agricultural dimension occupied mostly by automated facilities, League-owned but rarely visited except by maintenance personnel. Still, as off the beaten path and away from prying eyes as it was, transits out were heavily monitored. They would need to distract the League in a big way in order to gate out and hide somewhere with better amenities.

Alicia wasn't angry about his mistake; Walker seemed surprised about that, considering how good a friend Bob had been to her. But he didn't know about her feelings concerning his plan: a plan that required doing something she considered despicable. Fortunately, Kumai hadn't heard a word of it. And the nuisance of a conscience was easily remedied with circus.

On the night of the planned run, Kumai was understandably upset when she learned that Alicia had reneged on her promise to stop the circus. It took a generous dose of charm, and, subsequently, an even larger amount of stamina, but Alicia made it up to her for the better part of the night. She then slipped away as Kumai slept, peaceful and oblivious.

***

It was after she passed through the gateway to the Gaea transit station that Alicia realized to her chagrin she'd forgotten her OnBoard's module for Glossiu. This would be a terrible inconvenience, since her knowledge of language of this world was limited to some choice expletives, and –thanks to Kumai– a few phrases that were not exactly appropriate to be used in public. She knew that she could download a modular upgrade at a kiosk, but it would leave a trail to follow if the League were quick to react to her stunt. Purchases in her name would be too easy to trace, and she didn't want to risk using her fake IDs and credplates a second time. Her ONBoard had self-evolving language drivers, but it would just be a pain having to read from it, word for word, to decipher signs or speak with anyone, but after a moment of weighing her options, she decided that any purchases were too big a risk.

The fact that Gaea was Kumai's homeworld was the first of three things that made this job so despicable. Second was that it was so technologically backward, with computer systems and I-Link nodes had few to no defenses against hackers, making it a League protectorate in just about every possible way. And the third thing was Walker's choice of system to invade. Not only was

Tisvard the entire planet's main food distribution and management center; it was also Kumai's workplace. But Walker had been right in saying that hitting a vital axis plane of the League in the breadbasket would catch their attention. And it was specifically because Walker was calling the shots, that despite her better judgment, Alicia went along with his plan.

She set up shop in the cheapest hotel she could find, one that still allowed paper currency, which the League was gradually phasing out. Fortunately, the rooms were quite livable; there were no such thing as 'roach motels' in Gaea. She found that she needed a lot more circus than usual to go through with the mission, and by the time she'd boosted herself up with enough confidence by way of the drug, she felt like she was already online. The world was alive with the ghosts of I-Link colors superimposed upon reality, and she could barely feel her own fingers, let alone clearly speak her password. Still, she eventually managed to log on, and shunt herself into the network.

***

The run was too easy. The entire system was like something that I-Link tech would have interpreted systems out of the twentieth century to be, and the viral databomb she'd cast from her program arsenal through the e-mail script practically ate it alive. Afterwards, she set the viper within the trap, and waited in a nearby accounting construct maze. Its system structure was degraded from the databomb, but still fit for concealing her presence.

The prey came soon enough: first, a Gaean I-Link cop and then an enforcer. Usually the sight of the elite police/military of the League was enough to fill even the most overconfident criminal with terror, but Alicia simply laughed, the presence of circus erasing all natural fear. As a matter of fact, a part of her had been hoping for this: revenge for Bob. The League worked quickly, as expected. She'd expected an investigator or a higher ranking I-Link cop accompanying the Gaean, but this was much better.

Cloaked within Walker's shield program, anticipation wrenched her as the virus traps awakened and attacked, catching the two investigators unawares. Voracious data enzyme constructs herded the two into the proper place like a swarm of dog-sized ants, leaving a ragged mess of the node sector, and then vanished, confusing them as expected. The Gaean was the first to jack out, and Bob's Viper struck. Alicia had stifle an excited whoop. She'd hoped that the enforcer would have been the first to be hit, but it didn't really matter. Vipers jumped from one host to another, usually to whomever tried to remove them, and death was very slow and painful. There was no way to erase it; someone would die. It was simply a matter of who was hit first. Death took hours to days, though, and this would certainly catch the attention of more I-Link cops and enforcers who would try -and fail- to shut it down. Even if not, Alicia doubted that the circus would give her enough patience to watch the entire show. But she was already in her own world. Consumed with the thrill of the run and lust for revenge, and the high of circus, she'd already forgotten the job's true purpose.

Me-1, League-0, she whispered. *Rest in peace, Bob.*

Suddenly, every hair on the back of her neck rose. Something was wrong. Very wrong.

Though she'd never developed a sixth sense in the I-Link like Walker, a feeling of impending doom nevertheless sprang from out of nowhere and engulfed her like an ambush net. It weighed down upon her from all sides, robbing her of the edge of her doses of circus.

A man suddenly appeared beside the fallen I-Link cop. Not the luminescent monochrome of an avatar, but living, breathing, impossible color –Real. He was too far away to see clearly; the most prominent feature she could make out was the silver cloak that shrouded his body. As he gestured, she caught a glimpse of a hand, confirming that he was perhaps human, though without any certainty. Caught between alarm and fascination, Alicia watched as he removed the defensive programs from the enforcer who had returned, just as helpless as ever, and then, again performing the impossible, purged the virus from the dying I-Link cop, as if it were nothing. She then watched as he spoke briefly with the bewildered enforcer with words to low for her to hear, and then rippled away as if he'd just gated out.

The I-Link cop and enforcer, just as bewildered as she was, jacked out, their avatars vanishing in a shower of code, and leaving her alone.

Holy krid... Alicia blurted. *What the hell just...?*

In the middle of her thought, inexplicable pressure squeezed her on all sides. A sense utter panic consumed her, pressing upon her like the cold, agonizing embrace of an iron maiden. The neon world of the I-Link shifted, and she struggled to force down her gorge in the middle of a splitting headache. She needed to jack out, get back home, sleep, spend some time with Kumai...

Kumai.

Why did her thoughts have to return to her, and here and now, of all places?

Her squeaky voiced off-planer had most likely been right. Perhaps she'd been overdoing it on the circus after all. Maybe this was divine retribution for what she'd just done to her friend's homeworld and livelihood. If it was, God knew she deserved it. If she died here, how would she know? Alicia gritted her teeth nearly to breaking as anguished guilt finally flooded past the wall of circus-induced numbness. Fool that she was; she didn't leave a note or anything. Of course, what could she have said? "Sorry I had to leave our bed cold, Kumai, but I'm off to destroy your job and screw up your world's food supply; see you in the morning"?

Panic led to further panic when she tried to jack out, but was met with unexpected and frightening resistance. Like a tether to this electronic world, her systems were locked. Already present fear bloomed into terror. Alicia was almost certain her body was hyperventilating.

Then abruptly, everything froze.

Everything in the I-Link flowed, as energy and data moved from node to node, system to system, plane to plane. But somehow, impossibly, the pulsing flow of code in the system's scant constructs, including herself, was struck monochrome and cold.

Alicia screamed –and discovered, to her relief, that she could still do it. She'd expected sound to be as solid and silent as the datascape about her; instead, it echoed briefly into the otherwise silent and then, like someone quickly turning down the volume dial on a stereo system, faded away.

"I've invested too much time in this to let you get away before we've had a little chat, Ms. Barnes,"

The voice, slightly distorted through the gateway's event horizon, belonged to a man. Like someone gating in from the real world, a form rippled into existence.

The person who appeared was the same one she'd seen just a moment ago. He'd been too far away for her to get a good look at him before, but even up close, his features were obscured by a strange silver cloak. Of his face, all she could see were concealing dark shades and a thin stubble line from his lip to his chin. Nothing about him was familiar, yet he seemed to smile as if he knew her well.

What the hell do you want? Alicia said. Perhaps it was the vestiges of the circus, there was a numbness in her body that wiped away all previous fear. Hell was transformed temporarily into purgatory. *Who are you? Do you know what you just did?*

Saying nothing, he extended his right hand. Was he

trying to help her? But as his forearm, thick, bare, and sinewy, and encircled by three large metallic bracelets, emerged from the cloak's diaphanous ripples, what happened next quickly shattered this hypothesis.

The series of bracelets melted and joined together like smart quicksilver. The oddly flowing river of liquid metal then pooled into his palm and then extended solidly in either direction, taking the form of a long, cylindrical pole. The rear extension stopped at a length of a meter and a half, while the front grew forward and then outward, extending into a flat vane, poised at an odd curve.

Alicia's blood turned to cold mercury in its vessels when she recognized the shape.

The man lifted the device into the air, swinging upwards. Frozen like the world about her, Alicia felt her heart pounding furiously in the chest of her distant body.

Her question had barely a second to be asked, and was detached from her lips as the silver scythe came down upon her right shoulder.

In a jolt of static and pixels, and the scent and taste of blood, reality intruded in full color. Her body jerked upwards, but was held fast by a pair of strong hands. Alicia's chest involuntarily heaved and she retched, smattering someone's white medical frock with projectile vomit. Several alarms from unseen machinery were going off while voices barked orders in *Glossiu.*

A dull, sharp coldness hit her carotid artery, and she

blacked out.

***

Alicia's world was that of brief, fleeting periods of sometimes terrifying consciousness. The first was to the sight of shielded fluorescent lights shining in her eyes. The taste of blood was replaced with plastic and the sensation of an irritating sandpaper dryness in her mouth. More background voices spoke in Glossiu, but more subdued than before. Alicia tried to move her tongue, only to discover that a series of uncomfortable tubes prevented it. They ran down her throat and nose, making it impossible to talk.

A nightmare came to life as she turned her head in the direction of the arm that the I-Link stranger had hit with the scythe -or what would have been an arm, had it still been there. Instead, there was now little more than a bandaged stump.

Overwhelming grief combined with heart wrenching panic, hitting her like a right hook to the chest. Not her arm! Oh, God, please, not her right arm -her *playing* arm! Alicia squeezed her eyes shut, and prayed, willed, begged for this to not be real. Vision blurred and her eyes ran over with tears as her breaths came, shallow and rapid.

Monitors began to ring their shrill cadence of alarms. She jerked her body, trying to sit up, but strong hands again held her down. More alarms sounded, and the voices chattered more excitedly, still speaking in *Glossiu.* She saw a blue-skinned hand sheathed in white latex press a button on a machine below an IV of fluids, and her body became a lead weight. The world heaved and sounds became garbled and distant as she again felt the beginnings of a fall into unconsciousness. Rather than fight any more, she welcomed the oblivion, blessedly devoid of sensation, emotion, and memory.

***

Her next two awakenings were in the same location: a large tank of a strange thick, blue fluid that she found herself actually able to breathe, as if it were air. Her breaths came labored, the fluid inducing a feeling that was more like drinking rather than breathing. Each awakening, however, was short-lived, as someone sedated her. Nothing touched her; she simply became sleepy, as if something had been added to the fluid, and she passed out. Through both periods, however, Alicia recalled the stump that was her arm, and refused to look in that direction.

She did recall visitors during those two waking periods. And this was the worst pain of the entire experience. The first one was Kumai. Her image was distorted by the combination of fluid and glass in whatever tank that held her, but she recognized her pressed up against its surface. So she'd found her after all. God only knew how long it had taken her to discover where she was. It was obvious from the heavy pall of grief in her liquid black eyes that she knew something of what had happened. The tears on her face were so profuse, she could even see them through the distortion. She was sympathetic, and at the same time, ashamed in a way that made her feel worse than naked for the world to see, like she was already. But due to the fluid, found herself unable to cry.

The second visitor surprised her. In fact, it left her later wondering if she'd really seen what she thought she saw. She first recognized the black and gray nanomaterial enforcer uniform, which struck her with new fear and a plethora of questions, the chief of which being whether or not she'd been found out, and if she would be arrested. Then she saw the face, and instantly believed she truly was still asleep and dreaming, or that she'd lost her mind. The facial features were less rounded and more mature than she remembered, but it had, after all, been fifteen years. Still, she couldn't help but recognize her sister: the long, luxurious hair, the nose, closer to her mouth and smaller than her own, and the slightly elongated face lacking the star tattoo that had been applied to her own cheek.

Painful memories came back to her in that waking moment, buried ever since Walker had "died." Her parents were both Cybersoft techies, and both obsessed with their work and climbing the corporate ladder to the point where neither had much time for her or Kate in their childhood days. Still, they had high aspirations for both of them, perhaps too high. Kate was the "good" sister: always got the best grades and followed in their parents' footsteps; Alicia was the black sheep, always in trouble, and more interested in her own musical aspirations than her parents' wishes. Kate was obviously the choice sibling. They were close to each other as children, but drifted apart as their parents' duplicity became more obvious. In the end, she decided that if they liked Kate better, then they could have her. After that came memories of the kidnapping, the compound, and then Walker.

There were tears running down her face when she awoke -the first sign that she had been removed from the tank. All was silent, except the rhythmic bleeps from the heart monitor in the hospital room. She turned towards the outside window to see the pyramid-shaped buildings and two moons that confirmed she was both still in Gaea and Mezedia, but alone, as far as she could tell, in an insipid hospital room.

An unnatural breeze began to blow, moving from a blank wall on the opposite side of the room, towards the window —which was shut tight— instead of away from it. The wind was cold, and blew through the bed's flimsy blanket. Still weak from her series of ordeals and memories, Alicia struggled to turn her head in the opposite direction to see what was going on. She was too tired to feel fear, too spent to be worried, but curiosity managed to find strength enough to manifest itself.

A brief, *Now, what?* Flitted through her head as the silence of the room was shattered. The sound was like a heretofore unnoticed siren undergoing the Doppler Effect —only at a much lower series of pitches. The wall began to ripple and take shape as out of the distortion, a person came into view: another man, judging by the shape that manifested on the event horizon, and a chillingly familiar one at that. She recognized the silvery cloak instantly as he stepped forward and appeared, scythe first, the distorted event horizon of the now-obvious dimensional gateway reverberating and vanishing as he inserted his presence into this plane of reality, a silver-clad grim reaper.

"I know you," Alicia whispered, aware of, but strangely apathetic at her lack of fear. "Why did you take my arm?"

"Your arm was lost to begin with."

His voice, outside of the I-Link was deeper than she expected, even though she still couldn't completely make out his face. "You're far from a fool."

"Oh," was all she could say; she had no rebuttal for this. Even before she started using circus, Alicia had heard that overdoses did nasty things to your nervous system in weird places. He was wrong. She had been a fool, an ignorant, suicidal fool. She never once thought it could happen to her, or more specifically, her playing arm, but here she was, Alicia Barnes, A.K.A. Chevroness: one-time rock star-turned-drug statistic.

"Your brain was so addled with circus that you didn't know your front from your back," the man said. "I purged it from your system, but it was too late. It was all I could to do call an ambulance. If not for me, then you'd be dead."

For the first time since her second waking moment,

Alicia gathered the courage to shift her eyes towards the stump that was her right arm. It was heavily bandaged and fiber optic cables ran from it to a strange device on a white rolling cart. It looked like a desktop OnBoard set, but with a lattice of lights that shifted in psychedelic patterns where the switches would be. A noise that reminded her of a low-volume electronic whalesong emanated from it as streams of color and light went through hair-thin cable lines set at the right side of her bed.

"What is all this?" She said, at last finding her usual salt. "What do you want from me? Who the hell are you?"

"It's not what *I* want from you," the man said, placing the base of his scythe on the ground and twirling the handle in his hand. The silvery blade made a sharp hissing noise as it spun around and flashed strange colors in the light of the moons' light. "It's more a question of what we want from you."

Alicia made a disparaging cough. "Nice James Bond villain act there, man; but your creepy Merlin-with-no-beard routine needs a little work."

"Tell me, Miss Barnes," the man said, as if deaf to her snide remark, "what do you know of the MAGI?"

"So you're a terrorist?"

A wry grin cracked upon the side of the man's face. "Well, then, if you want to use that kind of logic, then one might say that you're a *terrorist* as well. And Kumai is your accomplice."

"You leave her out of this!" Alicia snapped. Even

though she raised her voice only slightly, a slight wave of dizziness overcame her. She moaned, bringing her remaining hand to cover her eyes as she rode out the wave of nausea. "Ugh ... Please, look, she had nothing to do with anything I did."

"I like your attitude," the man observed with some hint of bemusement. "You'll need it in your new life."

"In jail?"

"Why would you think that?" His surprise was genuine, and this was a great relief. So he wasn't an enforcer.

That was a surprise. Alicia half-expected when she woke up, to find her one arm in a brace and magna-locked to the bed's railing, along with a figure in the infamous black bodysuit sitting right across from her, waiting to drag her off to the League station holding cells, away from Kumai, away from Rax, away from Walker. Also, enforcers were known to have a flair for the dramatic only when they were chasing you, and this guy was hamming it up like nothing she'd seen before. "So you're not here to arrest me?"

"No. That comes later. Or to be more exact, it may come later. But that's definitely not up to me."

"Who are you?" Alicia gave her words a long, warning cadence as she made a show of her hand moving for the nurse's button.

"You needed to ask, sunflower?" The cloaked figure said. The voice was still the same octave, but the quality had transformed into something very familiar.

"No..." Alicia whispered.

The man passed his hand over the cloak that partially obscured his head. He then turned to the side, masking his face from her sight. But when he spoke again, the voice was a dead giveaway.

"You know who I am."

"Walker…"

"Tell me, do you love the League so much that you'll begrudge my saving your life at the expense of your arm?" He said, turning her way. His face was still hard to make out in the obscuring darkness, but then Alicia saw the telltale stripe of white, and large, toothy smile, "the same League that threw your band mate in prison on trumped-up charges? The same League that lied about his death to keep quiet about my own disappearance? The same League that killed your friend Bob?"

He removed the cloak from his face, bringing to light a smile that was not his usual jovial grin, but an expression that was more sinister, more obsessed. But he did not face her fully with this look, as if he dared not show this side of himself to her. It vanished like a cartoon irising out as he turned to face her. His expression was as grave and somber as that of the visage he wore when he gated into her room, but his voice was kinder and gentler than his face let on. "Sweetie, you'll forgive me for being out of your life, won't you?"

"I… Of course I will," Alicia said, her mind swimming and her heart awash with conflicting emotions. "Walker, what's going on? Are you for real? Are the MAGI for real? Are you really working for them? What do you mean the League killed Bob?"

"One question at a time," Walker warned, and then cast his face into an unreadable expression. "Short answers first. Yes, we're real, yes, I'm working for the MAGI, and yes, you've been had. The League killed Bob, and sent you to this world on that little job. You've been made into a pawn." He paused to sigh deeply. It was a sound heavy with regret. "And it's all my fault."

"How could it have been your fault?" Alicia said. "You're the best at what you do! I never-"

Walker placed his hand gently over her mouth. It was sheathed in white leather, and suffused with the spicy smell of his cologne that reminded her of their more innocent days together.

"Your words are flattering," Walker said, on the edge of laughter, "but I'm only human. I was monitoring the words the fake 'me' said to you on the tank; at least part of them were true. I *did* screw up. I underestimated the I-Link cops; with hackers like me, those bastards have the patience of Job. I guess some of them never really thought I was dead."

He paused long enough to give a rueful grin. "The second they got a taste of my style, they were hot on my ass, like green on grass. I thought I had anonymity on my side, but I was wrong. That's what led the operative to you. It was nothing to make you think I'd coaxed you here. The second I learned about it, I tried to get there before you could do some major damage and attract every enforcer in ten worlds, but I was too late. But the League's actions betrayed either their ignorance or arrogance; I'm not sure which. Either the operation was hush-hush from the higher-ups, or they only thought that one enforcer was enough. And then there was the fact that the enforcer didn't know what was in store. She walked right into that trap you set; I couldn't believe it myself. In addition, knowing who the enforcer was, scored two more points for our team, as it was none other than your sister."

Alicia said nothing to this, but the way she averted her eyes was obviously enough for Walker to draw a conclusion. "You two still aren't on speaking terms, I gather?"

"For fifteen years," Alicia said.

"Didn't I tell you to talk to her?" Walker said with an inflection of subtle reproach. "She was at least working for Cybersoft a couple of years ago. Now that she's an enforcer, who knows how much the League has brainwashed her? She may well arrest you without a moment's thought."

"What's it to you?" Alicia said, his words flaring a dormant anger within her. What was she saying? Goody-two-shoes or not, Kate was still her sister. Hell, she hadn't even gone to her parents' funeral after she'd learned of the lab accident that took their lives. What kind of a callous excuse for a human being had she become?

"She's *my* sister," she said, with less emotion than before. "Let me deal with her as I want."

"You might not have a choice in the matter," Walker said. "She found you out, after all."

"Oh god…" Alicia quavered. The waking moment in the fluid tank came back to her: the person standing there, whose features, though elongated and slightly distorted by the glass, were both familiar, and undeniable. Realizing that she hadn't been seeing things after all caused the full gravity of everything – what she nearly did in the I-Link, and who the enforcer was– to imbue her with new fear. "I nearly killed my own sister! And if what you said is true, then…"

"It's best not to assume," Walker said, being as comforting as pragmatism would allow. "Most likely, the bonds of blood are stronger than conditioning by the system. Who knows?"

"If you're trying to make me feel better, you're doing a piss-poor job," Alicia said, letting her resentment flow from every word. "And you still haven't told me what you want with me."

"I want you to play in your band, of course." Walker replied. At once, the scythe melted in his hand and the quicksilver enlarged and re-formed, ultimately solidifying into a silver Gibson Flying V electric guitar, complete with strings and frets. Its smooth, reflective surface shimmered hauntingly in the light of the moons, highlighting the word, *Sunflower*, engraved upon its surface.

"Play in my band, eh?" Alicia's voice was flat with scorn. "That's a frickin' laugh. That was my playing arm that got chopped off, there, genius. And I don't get enough royalties to afford a prosthetic."

Walker placed the guitar beside her bed, and then

gestured towards the mysterious machine attached to the remnants of her arm. "Who do you think funded this? Your arm is being injected with nanomachines in preparation for a prosthetic, one of the best ever made. But ..." he added the word with a peculiar emphasis, "... I have been told that there will be a price to be paid on your end."

"A price?" Alicia mulled over it in her head. She was never one to believe in urban legends, but tales of groups such as the MAGI were the stuff of actual legends. They opposed the worlds-spanning monopoly that was the League, and like djinns, they granted favors to whom they pleased, but required a sacrifice on the part of the recipient. God only knew why they'd tapped her, but more than anything, she wanted to be in the limelight once again. She wanted a life that she and Kumai could be proud of.

"Nothing good is ever free, eh?" Alicia said. "Is that what you're getting at?"

"Something like that." Walker made a slow, careful nod. "But our prices are neither exorbitant, nor unreasonable. Still, because you've caused such a need for fire control on our end, our price is twofold."

"Well, don't keep me waiting, honey," Alicia said. "Name it."

"First, you will get off the circus. Cold turkey; do not pass 'Go.'"

Alicia swallowed hard. Circus withdrawal was nothing pleasant to see, even worse to experience. But all things considered, it was really a small price to pay to have her arm back. "Agreed," she said. "What's the second?"

"You work for us, now."

"Doing what?"

"Whatever we need. You wanted revenge for Bob, right? Revenge for me and Rax? This time, you'll be doing it right."

"And that's it?" Alicia said. "It's just that easy?"

"It's never easy, sweetheart." Walker shook his head grimly. "I learned that long ago. But it's rewarding."

"Is that what you meant by my new life?"

Walker nodded.

"No other way?"

"Not unless you want to be the second amputee in the Rock n' Roll Hall of Fame."

In for a penny, in for a pound. Alicia sighed, finding that it was all that she could do. Still, in the end, she found the choice to be an easy one. "Okay. Agreed."

"Done, then." Walker then turned and glanced briefly at the door. There was noise on the other side, voices speaking not in *Glossiu*, but English. "This is where I leave you, sunflower," he said, and leaned over her.

Alicia felt his lips upon hers, but it wasn't like the kisses they shared their halcyon days. This was a simple goodbye, giving little more than a sweet memory of their past. It was brief, but left her with a dazed smile as she watched Walker merge into the wall and ripple away. His words, "I'll see you around," echoed through the gateway, distorted, and then vanished.

She barely had time to absorb all that had just happened when the door opened. In spite of her confusion and uncertainty over all that had transpired, Alicia could not stop the tears from flowing when she saw her sister appear, still clothed for work, and with Kumai close behind.

"You have a guest," the nurse said, her Glossiu words superimposed with a digitized voice that translated. Kate entered with an initial expression of busy annoyance, which melted instantly as their eyes met —both steel gray, and with the telltale look of their Asian heritage. She paused, and then begin to cry herself.

"I didn't believe it," she whispered between tears, her soft voice shaky with barely gated emotion. "I… I thought it was a lie. Oh, Aly… is it really you?"

"Yeah." Alicia couldn't help but smile through her own torrent of tears. "Hi there, Katie. It's your screw-up sister."

Kate practically fell to her knees beside the bed, and gently took Alicia's head in her arms. The bodysuit she wore smelled more like motor oil than the leather that its texture reminded her of. "Aly…" She heard Kate sniffle wetly. "Mom and dad thought … *I* thought you were dead! Why the hell didn't you let me know?"

"Geez, Katie? You don't watch the tank?" Alicia rolled her eyes. "I was only on it about fifty million times."

Kate stopped, and then gazed at her, genuinely confused at first. Her eyes narrowed in thought as she inspected her face.

"Chervroness?" Alicia said, amazed, and yet determined to jog her sister's memory, "from Ambush; that ring a bell? I thought you loved rock music."

"Things change after fifteen years," Kate said. "I don't go man-hunting to the clubs every night like I used to —not that it did me much good." She let go of the embrace, wiping the tears from her cheeks with one hand, while the other brushed back Alicia's noticeably shorter, purple-highlighted hair. "Look at you; you look like krid."

"I'm getting better."

Kate tried to suppress a laugh, but failed. Alicia followed, and soon, the two shared the first conniption fit they'd had in fifteen years.

***

Kate said that she had to leave in a hurry before her lateness attracted unwanted attention from the League brass, but promised to see her again. Alicia smiled. She knew now that Kate had known what had happened on the I-Link, and was taking a big risk hiding her from prying eyes. She regretted that it took fifteen years for a reunion. She only hoped that next time they met, she would have a second arm to embrace her with.

Kumai, who had been in the room, silent, while she and Kate shared their reunion, came forward, moved a chair from the wall beside the window, and sat by the head of her bed. Her black eyes, ever unreadable, seemed to partly gaze down at her, partly stare into nothingness as she took hold of Alicia's remaining hand. Perhaps choosing her words carefully, as Gaeans were wont to do, she was silent for a long while before at last deciding to speak.

"Despite the disarray of the company, Kumai has been given time off while you recover. Kumai is glad to see that you have survived, tir-Alicia."

"I'm sure you're pissed that I didn't keep my promise," Alicia said. "Don't hold back on my account."

Kumai was silent. Eerily so.

"And ... I understand if you ... y'know, want to leave."

A tear flowed down her pale blue cheek from her solid black iris. "No, tir-Alicia! Why would Kumai leave?"

"After all the krid I stirred up? After the circus?" Alicia hefted herself to her side. "You'd still want to hang around a loser like me? I mean, I'm glad, blueberry; I really am. And I promise it's cold turkey with the circus; I swear. But I caused so much trouble for you. I know most humans would call it quits after that.

With a smile, Kumai brushed Alicia's hair from her face. To Alicia, that expression spoke volumes more than any words she had to say.

"You are tir-Alicia. That will never change. But Kumai hopes that you have learned a lesson."

Alicia swallowed. God, her throat felt dry. "Oh, I have; believe me, I ain't touching the stuff again. I mean it. I really do. She managed to wave the stump of her right arm. "I paid the price. I'm not letting it take more body parts. Gonna get off of the circus for good."

Like her sister had done, Kumai pulled her into an embrace of her own, only tighter. She heard her give an elated sigh. "Oh, tir-Alicia! Kumai is so happy! Kumai will help you to get well. Kumai will be with you all the way."

"Yeah… thanks." Alicia's voice was choked to a rasp by the Gaean's surprisingly strong grip. "Now could you let go? Even humans have to breathe, you know."

Kumai gasped and broke away, covering her mouth gingerly with her hands. "You are not well yet!" She squeaked, her lips and nose shielded by her slender fingers. "Kumai is sorry!"

Weakly, Alicia rolled onto her back. Lifting her left arm, she brought it to Kumai's cheek, watching as her wide eyes softened and her blue skin once again turned blushed to a soft lilac color. Alicia smiled, managing her same mischievous sparkle in her eyes, despite her sudden onset of exhaustion.

"You really are cute when you're scared; you know that?"

***

Detox was hell —not that Alicia didn't expect it to be. The doctors told her that circus withdrawal was the worst, but she hadn't quite believed them, not until the onset of the pain and tremors, and then she experienced both in their full, hellish fury. Her memories were hazy, but she knew that Kumai kept by her side through the intense pain in her eyes, throbbing headaches, muscle spasms, and false I-Link hallucinations. Such was the devotion of Gaeans: something she was truly thankful for, because she was certain she'd thrown up on her at least three times in the process. Still, it was all necessary; the doctors wouldn't dare fit her new arm unless all the drugs were out of her system.

Once she was clean, the surgery was done. With her nerves all connected to the installed prosthetic's nanofibers, it was as if she'd never lost her arm at all. Alicia breezed through physical therapy, amazing every doctor who worked with her, and a month later, she was back to playing her guitar with the skill she'd always possessed.

But rebuilding a band took more time than she'd first expected. Several months passed before she could gather the courage to bring Rax out of hiding. Kumai did the rest, working with a few esoteric doctors on Gaea who specialized in the physiology of the few off-planers who trafficked in their world in order to alter him enough to pass for human. Rax was understandably indignant at losing his facial horns, but soon grew accustomed to the change. Besides, it was far preferable to rotting in prison again. As far as the public was concerned, Rax was dead, and would have to remain that way. The official story was that Ambush had merely picked up a new drummer and was starting from scratch.

. For a time, hers was a full apartment once she'd taken Rax –now "Rick" in the public eye– off of Walker's hands. Kumai had taken to staying at her own home in Gaea more often, in order to give herself some breathing space, but the plus side was that whenever she did choose to crash on Earth, Alicia always made it worth her while. Despite the rocky start, Alicia and Rax –with Kumai's help– managed to get hold of T.J. -also gone into seclusion, and more than happy to re-start the band-, pull strings with their agent and label, and get the wheels in motion for a reunion tour. It was a success beyond their wildest dreams. Ambush was put back on the map.

***

Kate visited for their tour's final stop on Earth.

"You know, once I had the chance to look it up, I realized that I did listen to your group after all," she said as she removed the beer from the dispenser in the dressing room, "a lot, as a matter of fact. I was a real big fan for a time, back when I was working at Cybersoft. I just never knew it was you."

"I still can't believe you didn't," Alicia said. She gave a rueful guffaw that forced a tiny bit of her own beer into her nose before she could swallow, causing her to sneeze. "I knew I wore a lot of makeup on stage, but I didn't think that my own sister wouldn't recognize me."

"Well, remember, the last time I saw you, you were shorter, and your hair was longer," Kate reminded her. "But then again, I guess maybe that was why I liked your group so much. Maybe deep down inside, a part of me knew that you were my sister. You just didn't look like the one I remembered." She glanced over Alicia with a scrutinizing eye, and cast her a lopsided grin. "You still don't, come to think of it."

"That was a lifetime ago, Katie," Alicia said absently, all the while fumbling with her silver guitar: her only proof thus far that what had happened in the hospital on Gaea hadn't been another circus dream. The instrument sure played like a dream, though; that was a certifiable fact. It was as if the guitar and her new arm had been made for each other. She ran her fingers over the engraved sunflower upon its surface and smiled. A brief warm feeling came to her chest as she zipped the satchel closed.

"Well, you seem to be doing well for yourself," Kate said as they came out of the dressing room. "A dream come true, just like you told me."

"Yeah, well, I need to survive this tour first," she said, lugging the satchel onto her back. "It's already kicking my ass, and though Kumai isn't saying anything, she's feeling the burn too. And we got three worlds left on this thing; we're gonna be so spanked by the time we get back to Earth."

"Well, I know I'm just family, but if you want my opinion, I think you rocked the house five times over tonight. I wouldn't be surprised if doctors tomorrow have a surplus of patients from the audience, with laryngitis and busted eardrums."

"Well, that's encouragement if I've ever heard it," Alicia said with a laugh. "Ah, but what about you?" She eyed her sister with hurried concern, but there was no way to be tactful about it. She hadn't seen Kate in months. "About that night, I mean. Your head was on the chopping block on my account?"

"Not really," Kate said –much to her sister's relief. "There was some ruckus at HQ, but it got bogged down in red tape before long. Just make sure that krid you pulled was a one-time-only thing."

"Trust me, Katie, you won't have to worry about that," Alicia said. They reached the fork in the pathway outside the stadium. One led to Alicia's ride –out of the way of the more tenacious fans gathered at the main exit, and the other led to the nearly empty parking lot, where Kate's motorcycle waited. She turned and gave her sister a final hug goodbye. "You sure you gotta leave so soon? There's room for one more roadie, you know." Her eyes sparkled with the mischief that Kate had so well remembered from their childhood. "We got a lot of catching up to do, you and I."

Kate's smile faded. "That's true," she said, and then sighed resignedly, "but for now, we live on two different worlds, Aly. Our paths will have to cross whenever fate gives us a chance. I got a job to do, and you have yours."

"True," Aly said wistfully. "So very true. Well, Katie, I guess it's goodbye for now. Don't be a stranger, you hear?"

"I'll keep in touch," Kate said and started off down her path. "Break a leg, sis."

Alicia waved goodbye, watching until her sister rounded the far end of the stadium, out of sight.

"Does she know?" Walker said, appearing behind her. She didn't start; it had become a commonplace thing since he'd first made contact.

"You weren't listening in?" Alicia said, not looking behind her.

"I just like to be thorough." The odd fabric of Walker's cloak shimmered ethereally in the light as it gently billowed in a breeze that only it could feel.

"I thought she had something to do with your plans."

"All in good time. You come first. And you've done a good job."

"Haven't I, though? Y'know, sometimes I surprise myself," Enjoying her bravado, Alicia touched the small groove in the wrist of her artificial arm. She could feel the nanofibers inside the compartment –a special addition by the MAGI, undetectable by conventional medical scanners–, coiled and ready to subsume more systems like she had been doing for the last few months, as per Walker's instructions. It all seemed so random, however: an I-Link terminal here, a traffic box there, and sometimes even an e-menu or two at fast food chains. Of course, they were all League-owned, used on Earth and on a hundred different worlds, but there was no pattern. What did it add up to? "So, you care to tell me what the grand scheme is thus far?"

"You're doing well so far, sunflower. To bring down a behemoth, one does not attack full-on, but little by little, chipping away at foundations. You play a part in a larger scheme. And both anonymity and partial ignorance are your protection. After all, though there are plans for your sister, she's not yet a part of this. And being that she's an enforcer, she is not one that either you, or I, want to make an enemy of."

"Can't argue with you there," Alicia said, her words coaxing a smile from Walker's tattooed face, the first she had seen in a long time.

As he'd done so many times before, Walker pressed the disk into the palm of her artificial hand, and instantly, the nanofibers wrapped around it and dragged it, half-melting, inside her arm. The sensation was indescribable, but something she'd become accustomed to. She didn't fight it as she first had, with notably painful results; rather, she now let the process happen, allowed the data to integrate itself into her mind, flowing piece by piece into her long-term memory, as if she'd learned a vocal text to recite. She was now the bearer of a set of instructions and code that made as little sense to her as her other assignments.

"Your next assignment," Walker said. "Do you understand it?"

"Yes, and no," Alicia said.

"Good answer," Walker nodded cordially. "See you around, sweetie."

This was going to be an interesting tour.

He vanished just as Kumai's voice began to call

her name. She hurried down the path and arrived at the waiting magcar. The words, *AMBUSH REUNION TOUR: THE ATTACK IS BACK!*, were painted in stylized red and white letters on its black stainless steel chassis.

"We have to go, tir-Alicia," Kumai said, taking the guitar satchel and stuffing it into the luggage compartment of the magcar. "The tour must remain on schedule."

A burning pain sliced through her artificial arm as she grabbed the railing on the magcar's entrance hatch. Alicia froze, and sucked in a breath of air through her teeth. Not again. This was the fifth time this week that it started hurting. She at first had been afraid that it was the nanofibers or the downloads, but it had come during times long after or long before her rendezvous with Walker, meaning it was just a mundane glitch. But it had become annoying, and this was the last straw. She didn't care what the medtechs said; something was funky with the connections on this thing. Next stop, she was hitting a hospital before the concert. Screw the notoriety; it was hurting like hell.

"Your arm still hurts?" Kumai said, both concerned for her and eager for the magcar to get underway. Though fuel was a non issue for this type of vehicle, the League was downright anal when it came to times for gateway transfers, and this one had to be made in orbit to get to the world which was the band's next stop. Timing would be especially of the essence.

"I'll live," Alicia said. "I can still play the guitar,

and that's good enough for me."

"You play just as well as Kumai remembers," Kumai said. "You must be happy, now that your band's music has made the charts."

"Yeah, but it's messed up that I had to lose an arm to see the big picture," Alicia said.

"At least you no longer do circus," Kumai said. "Kumai is happy about that."

"It wasn't my idea."

"Kumai is sorry."

"Forget it," Alicia gave a reassuring smile. "I'm not sensitive about it, or anything."

She never did tell Kumai all that had happened; perhaps the off-planer knew that she was hiding something, but some things were better left unsaid, and she never asked. Still, Alicia needed her, and she hoped they needed each other. And Kumai was a very capable manager. T.J. was back, along with Rax, plastic surgery and gene therapy safely obscuring his identity, and Ambush was now on the road to a comeback.

"Back on the road again," she said to no one but herself, before she turned to Kumai. "You know, blueberry, I can't tell you how much I missed this life."

Alicia collapsed into the sofa bed in the back cabin and shut her eyes. The pain in her arm was gone. Kumai sat beside her, and leaned onto her shoulder, falling almost instantly into a light slumber, equally exhausted. Alicia made a tiny hum at the sight of her. She was cute even when she wasn't worried.

###

78

79

Psyche

Today was Friday, the end of her standby shift. This meant that Kate would be shuffling off her uniform for the weekend. Though there was never any real reason to take it off -nanomaterial could mimic any fabric and was self-cleaning-, on some paranoid level, a part of her felt like she was not so much in control of it, as it was trying to take over, like she was in a constant battle of wills against the A.I. that governed its components. What worried her most was how it resisted whenever she did remove it, as if it hated her for rejecting the comfort and protection it provided. It felt like pinpricks in each of the pores of her skin, as if hanging on for dear life, making a conscious effort to remain on her, even after she gave the mental "release" command.

It was a fear she only shared with Dr. Galt, the League psych evaluator. What a coincidence that her train of thought would swerve in this direction during an evaluation. And no doubt Dr. Galt would pick it up, either on the brain scan running through her biocomp or on his own, being the off-planer and psychic that he was.

"Tried to sneak away from our little session again, have we?" The doctor asked in his slightly exaggerated, almost-German accent. The chief had to have told him about her previous attempts at shirking her appointments; it was the only way he could have known. She had hoped that she could have done so again, but the chief liked to keep a tight leash on his subordinates. The reminder popped in her field of vision today just as she had finished lunch: priority one, mandatory. The doctor was kind enough, but his voice, for its out-of-place accent, was oily, snake-like, and did little to endear him to her. But she bore him no ill will; after all, he did go out of his way to be nice.

"I hope it wasn't because of me." The doctor rubbed his tiny hands together as one of the four pseudopods that grew from his hunched back manipulated the readouts upon the touch screen of his OffBoard peripheral.

"No. Not you," A flat, mildly sarcastic tone managed to escape her voice, even though she was being earnest. "You'll excuse me if I don't like you probing into my head."

"Oh, surely it's not so bad," Dr. Galt protested, with a laugh that was just as dissonantly unsettling as his voice. "Procedure and all that, especially when you've got so many bionics attached to you."

"Yeah. Procedure," Kate echoed, unable to move much more than her arm to bring the cup of Darjeeling tea to her lips. Tendrils of nanofiber ran like cascades of straight black hair from her uniform, wove together at their ends like braids, and were shunted into multiple jacks on several terminals. All there was left was to sit and wait while the doctor took his readings. "Thanks for the tea, by the way."

The doctor nodded cordially, and continued his work. No questions were asked; there was no need. He could see inside her mind as easily as he could see readouts from her OnBoard as it fed data into his brain via the INplant at his right temple. And this composed the entirety of the evaluation in all its inane boredom.

"Seems that everything is in order," the doctor said at last, stirring Kate from her state of between-sleep-and-awake. He touched a key sequence on his periphery, and the tendrils retracted from the terminals, flowing like a river running on rewind, into her suit's mass reservoirs with an audible snap. The empty teacup rattled in her hands upon its saucer. "And that will be all for me … until next month, that is."

With little more than a noncommittal sound, Kate rolled out of the couch. Her steps were ungainly at first, but her biocomp quickly compensated as it awoke from standby mode. She managed a brief smile at the doctor as she left the office, but had no intention of showing up next month. And to make sure that the chief would not call her out on it, she planned to have a talk with Jackie about the League mainframe, schedules, and the fudging thereof.

The ghost of an itch ran across her skin. She scratched reflexively. God, she would be glad to get this thing off, and move around without digital checks and balances made on her every bodily function! Now, there was only a brief detour for calibration and diagnostics, and then she would be home sweet home, enjoying beer and barbecue packs.

Kate paused, suddenly as a ping ran through her biocomp and caused a tremor in her skin. The words, PRIORTIY MESSAGE: REPORT TO DIRECTOR GARRETT, shone in bright red, flashing their urgency in her line of sight.

"Damn," Kate said under her breath. Had he started reading her thoughts now?

It was worse, she discovered all too quickly.

"Your regular shift has been extended." The director had said the words she dreaded. Her insides were one part a lead weight, and one part seething with vitriol. But she maintained a steady poker face; duty first, after all. It was always duty first with the League, but she could not help the thoughts that ran unbidden through her mind.

What the hell are you thinking?

Do you have any idea how much I look forward to taking this thing off?

Don't you have about a hundred other A-Class enforcers on tap?

"What's the assignment?" Was what she asked.

"The MAGI," Garrett said. "I'm sure you heard of them?"

With a thought, Kate's biocomp scoured the I-Link and supplied her with the relevant data about the organization. There was, surprisingly, very little. They were considered a terrorist group by the League simply because they opposed them (paranoid much?). Their list of "sins" consisted mostly of data infiltration and industrial espionage on some pretty sophisticated mainframes.

Kate frowned as her feelings of indignation deepend to something that was almost like hatred. This was grunt work, pure and simple, and far beneath an A-class. "What's wrong?" She asked, disguising her disdain under a veneer of snide stoicism, "techies can't handle a few super hackers? Finally caught one in the real world, and you need me to babysit him?"

"No."

Oh, right. Humor and sarcasm were completely wasted on the director. His tone was as flat as yesterday's soda, colorless as his office: no plaques, pictures, or personal effects of any kind, save the League half-star symbol, mounted prominently behind him in brass behind his featureless mahogany desk. The man was practically a robot.

He touched a sequence on his OffBoard, and Kate's biocomp signaled an upload with a shrill chirp. Immediately, data integrated itself with her memories.

"Those are your orders," the director said with finality as a familiar name stood out the data. The face to match that name suddenly came through the door, her blue skin and snow-white hair unmistakable.

"Mukai?" Kate rose from her chair quickly to greet her friend. "When did you come back to Earth?"

Mukai smiled kindly and bowed. "An hour ago. It is good to see you again, friend Kate. I look forward to working with you." She spoke in Glossiu, the language of her world, meaning her INplant had not been outfitted with an English translation matrix. Her transfer to Earth had indeed been a swift one.

"She will be working with you on this case," the director announced.

"You're joking, right?" Kate quipped. Perhaps no English module was a good thing, she thought, or else Mukai might have taken her words as an insult. She gave her a quick glance, but Mukai's decorum was better than a marine's.

"No. She has the technical expertise you will need. And you two have had a good, albeit brief working history, and a longer personal history. You know this is a good pairing, Lieutenant."

"Krid," Kate swore under her breath. Robot though the director might have been, he was always right.

***

Their first stop was supposed to be at an ATM across town, but a realtime update had changed their destination to the old transcontinental Bridge: an abandoned project from the more optimistic previous century, where squatters had set up a miniature city over the years. Apparently, a new suspected access had been made at a local restaurant that she was familiar with, but details, as expected, were sketchy. Mukai had always been few of words, but she had obviously never driven a car through subspace; the way she flinched as the ghosts of traffic passed harmlessly through their car where there should have been lethal collisions was amusing, but not unexpected. Subspace was the best way to travel if one were in a hurry. Kate found herself unable to suppress a laugh as Mukai staggered out of the car onto the parking lot, making profuse apologies. Kate reassured her friend that her disorientation was normal, and then led the way up to the shops, bazaars, parlors and dives on the Bridge's second tier.

"First time on enforcer business?" Kate asked. Though Mukai wore no English translation matrix, Kate had one for Glossiu, though she knew the language fairly well. Still, a matrix helped for the big words.

"It is my first time directly working with one on Earth," Mukai said with a nod.

"Well, it's good to have someone helping, even if you're an import," Kate admitted. "I mean I don't know what could've possessed the director to deputize an off-planer from a completely unrelated organization, but..." Her voice trailed off as they neared their destination down the crowded thoroughfare, its old sign suspended from overhanging rooftops.

That was when she realized that the sign was actually on. The unusualness of this alone gave her pause to just stare. The name "Pink's" shone in neon cursive, the same color as the name, as if it had never spent those last ten years burned out and unrepaired.

"Under new management it seems," Kate observed aloud, then saw that the windows of the facade had been repaired, and a fresh coat of varnish graced the entrance door. Even the latch was new, shining with the near-gold sheen of polished brass, where the old one was rusted solid and had barely been hanging onto the door frame.

She stepped inside, and the unexpected and pleasant scent of newness and sawdust greeted her. The place looked like some itinerant fairy had taken up light housekeeping reversed the effects of time. The many and sundry photos of the music groups who played there in the past were still posted on the walls, but amidst a backdrop of fresh white paint newly applied to the sheetrock, free of yellowing and graffiti; the furniture, tables, menus and order terminals were also brand new.

"If I wasn't on duty…" Kate said. With a wistful sigh, she steeled herself for the task. ahead.

"We'll be checking the order terminals first," she told Mukai. After showing her credentials to the surprised, but acquiescent manager, she set to work.

During the investigation, Kate realized, much to her chagrin, that she was hungry –small wonder there, since the director hadn't given her the opportunity to grab a snack before heading out, and she was long overdue for dinner. And that the VIRsense matrix encoded into the order terminals for OnBoard access did not help to diminish her appetite. Soon, after being bombarded by the simulated sights and smells of a hundred menu items, she could stand no more. She jacked out of the system and located Mukai, who was now five rows down and still hard at work. I'll leave her to it, she thought, personally wanting to just get away from the torment of food.

She snapped the terminal's face plate back into place as her jack retracted back into her suit, then prepared to make an order for something to drink while the investigation continued, still decidedly, annoyingly unfruitful.

A minute later, she was sipping on a glass of iced Green Dream, inputing parameters of real world legwork into her biocomp. She was admiring the finished half of the ongoing repair job on the rear stage, when she noticed someone appear from behind the curtains.

"Hey!" Kate hurried down the way, and through the barricades that warned of the danger. "That's a microbot area; get out of there. You could mess up their programming; they might turn this whole Bridge into-"

She paused in her tracks as she approached the stage, and then slowed to a walk. A smile had erupted upon her face, as well as the face of the person across the way.

"Aly!"

"Sis!"

Kate's mind went back to a conversation with a coworker from about three years ago, and the photo that accompanied it, still hanging on the wall above the booths in the eating area. She had been right. Alicia did look almost exactly like her, but with shorter hair, highlighted in purple, and with a star tattooed beneath her left eye. It had been years since they'd seen each other, until they were reunited during an investigation in Mukai's home dimension of Gaia nearly two years ago Kate's younger sister grinned as she sat on the edge of the stage, her legs dangling. She wore all black, and for a moment, Kate thought it was another enforcer uniform. But as her sister reached out and took her hands, and then hopped to the floor where they shared a happy embrace, she noticed that there were no line patterns or half star insignia -then it dawned on her that it was a diffusion suit, for safe interaction with on-duty microbots.

"Nice coinkeydink, meeting you here," Alicia said.

"I used to come here all the time, actually," Kate replied. I actually saw you perform a few times, back before you went platinum."

Alicia sighed as she ran her gaze across the breadth of the stage, the billions of microbots still hard at work, doing repairs one molecule at a time, un-rotting the wood, re-weaving and re-coloring the curtains, and un-rusting the metal. "Yeah, it brings back memories; that's for sure. Broke my heart when I came back from tour and saw the kridpile this place had become."

"Well then," Kate said, "if you're not the luckiest girl in all the worlds. Seems like the new owner liked this place the way it used to be."

Alicia gave a wry grin. "Who do you think bought it?"

Kate gave an explosive laugh that surprised even her. "You're kidding! "You bought this dump?"

"Won't be a dump for long," Alicia said. "Soon, this'll be the hottest night spot on the Bridge."

"No krid?" Kate scanned over the half-completed

stage, a jarring contrast of decay and newness being born from dilapidated sections. "New sounds like before?"

"Revue of up-and-coming talents from every plane known to man and off-planer."

Kate couldn't help but grin. It was like the nanobots had rearranged the muscles on her face. "Wow. So I guess you've been busy since the last time I saw you,"

"That was a year ago," Alicia reminded her.

"A year ago?"

"Yep."

"Seriously?"

Alicia nodded. "Time flies, sis, and it just flew right by you."

"So, should I say that 'Chevroness' dumped Ambush to strike out on her own?

Alicia spat air from her lips. "When we're up for a Grammy? You wish. We're just taking a little break. The tour was rough; you ever been to Shenijen? Laws of physics are bass-ackwards crazy there; makes our music sound way different. And that's not the only world like that, you know. By the end of our tour, my migraines were starting to have baby migraines."

"And now you're going to start a club for amateurs?" Kate laughed. "I fail to see how that's going to relax you, but whatever floats your boat, sis. Good luck with that."

Alicia gave an abrupt and infectious start when the powerful green light suddenly appeared in corner of Kate's eye, and then moved across her field of vision.

Kate winced reflexively, and her eyes trailed the beam to a device held by Mukai, who had appeared almost out of nowhere.

"God, Mukai, you almost made me piss my uniform!" Kate exclaimed, and then exhaled in relief. Her biocomp registered the beam as a combination of magnetic waves used in brain scans, and then suggested a mild sedative injection, which she refused. "Wait," she glanced back to the rows of booths, a nearly impossible notion appearing in her mind, and just as soon dismissed. "You can't possibly be finished checking all those booths already."

"I am." Mukai gave a very casual nod, as if such a feat were nothing. She then pointed her device towards Alicia, who flinched slightly as the green light passed over her.

Kate had been about to protest; technology-wise, Gaea was a slightly backwater world, but then her biocomp brought information of the League's new labor exchange program, which Garrett's data said that Mukai was a part of, to mind. And even in her home dimension, she had been damn good at her work.

A shrill chirp came from Mukai's device.

"A match in brainwave/OnBoard algorithms," Mukai explained before Kate could ask. Her friend cast her liquid black-eyed gaze directly towards Alicia. "*She* is who we are looking for."

"Wh…Who-?" Kate sputtered at the news, which had not quite registered in her mind, but slowly, like a slow data feed from her biocomp, began to clarify in frightening detail. "I mean what the-? You can't be … *Her*? No, no, no!"

Her biocomp flashed several accelerated heart rate warnings as she yanked the device from Mukai. Her suit was capable of performing brain scans of its own, but she had to prove that the programming of Mukai's scanner was faulty. There was no way her sister could be their target. From her hand, tendrils of nanofibers slithered into the device's transmitter, which fed the readouts into her field of vision. The uniform adapted to the device's programming and then released a diode which protruded from her shoulder and scanned Alicia, who stood like a deer frozen in headlights. As it had on the device, it came back positive.

Suddenly cold all over, Kate backed away from her sister, her steps halting and trembling as Mukai placidly watched on. How the hell could her own sister be MAGI? This seemed a nightmare of multiple levels of wrongness. Her voice was a pained groan when she finally spoke. "No. God, Aly … why?"

Her expression as immutable as Mukai's, Alicia stepped forward. She opened her mouth to speak, but whether it was to deny or explain, Kate never knew, as several things happened at once.

The air grew colder, and Kate knew that it was not because of her emotional state, especially when a buzz and priority message from her biocomp issued the alarm.

WARNING. MULTIPLE SUBSPACE RIFTS

DETECTED.

Kate tensed inwardly, but loosened her body to a combat-ready stance. She felt the weapons forming in her uniform's mass reservoirs, but refrained from ejecting them.

How many? She sent the thought to her biocomp.

NINE RIFTS TOTAL. LEAGUE I.F.F. SIGNAL CONFIRMED IN FIVE: FOUR, FIVE, SIX, SEVEN, AND EIGHT O'CLOCK FROM CURRENT POSITION. SIGNAL NEGATIVE AT ELEVEN, TWELVE, TWELVE-THIRTY, AND ONE O'CLOCK FROM CURRENT POSITION.

The air —no, it was space itself— rippled from behind and in front of her, and behind where Alicia stood. From the rifts in back, a small force or C-class enforcers appeared, armed with magnetic rail rifles, and shielded with thick spidersilk vests and black helmets. A clear spark of consternation flashed through Kate in the midst of her conflicting emotions. Having backup unrequested, and with this much overkill in weaponry, showed a complete lack of faith on the director's part. Garrett well knew that an A-class was more than capable of bringing in one girl, her sister or not.

But then, the beings who stepped out of the rifts behind Alicia snuck doubt into her confidence. Their silver cloaks confused her for a moment, but as their forms clarified once they emerged from the event horizon, they were quite different: off-planers all, each from a different dimension. One was female, green-skinned, and with hair that looked like electrical wiring.

Another was ethereal and fairy-like, with wings that folded over her willowy features, honey blonde hair, and cloak, like sparkling veins running through its diaphanous material. Another was wide-bodied and brutish, like a werewolf and gorilla mixed together, while another had a face so heavily tattooed, it was impossible to determine anything at all about him.

"Hey now… no need to get hostile, sis," Alicia said, making a gentle placating gesture —one the enforcers responded to with the harmonized crescendo of their weapons' accelerators powering up.

"Stand down!" Kate ordered, giving a stern gesture to the enforcers. But they held their positions. Kate gaped, half in irritation, half in fear.

"They won't listen to you," the green-skinned one said in an unexpectedly high voice. "Their orders come from the director himself."

"W- what do you want?" Kate demanded, the fingers on her gloved hand extending into claws, and retracting in response to her confusion. She pointed at Alicia and the assembled MAGI. Were they MAGI? There was no way to know, but her gut instinct practically screamed an affirmative. "You've never appeared anywhere en masse."

"Haven't we?" Green Skin said, almost amused.

"What's going on, then?" Kate demanded. "Why is my sister one of you?"

"This isn't what you think," Alicia said in a calm, but stern voice. "In fact, nothing you see here is."

"Not your job, not the League… Your whole life

after Cybersoft has been practically a lie," Green Skin said.

"How do you know about Cybersoft?" Kate said, ignoring the foolishness of that question. It didn't take a hacker to find out her job history, after all. "Aly, please! Why are you with them?"

"I've always been with them," Alicia replied matter-of-factly. "Katie, there's so much we want to tell you, but … now's not the time, you know? And they know too much already."

"'They'? Who are 'they'?" Alicia said, and swallowed hard against a dry throat.

"The League," Green Skin replied.

"We can tell you more later," Alicia said.

"Enough talk," Mukai said, boldly stepping towards Alicia, as if the assembled MAGI were invisible to her. She reached into the obi sash of her uniform and removed a pistol.

"Mukai, what the hell are you doing?" Kate said through gritted teeth. Her biocomp made a series of shrill medical warnings which she effectively silenced with a thought.

"She must be arrested, or terminated," Mukai said.

"Are you out of your freaking mind?" Kate exclaimed. "That's my sister; there's no way in hell you're going to kill her!"

"We have our orders, friend Kate."

"No. My orders," Kate said with finality. "With all due respect, Mukai, you're not an enforcer; you're a …" she paused as her translation matrix sought the correct word in Glossiu, "… a 'techie'." She shifted her gaze back to her sister. "Aly. Come with me to League HQ; we can talk about this. If worse comes to worst, my lawyers can defend-"

Mukai's gunshot echoed in the restaurant, and in Kate's mind, it became the only sound, fragmented by the image of horror that broke her: Alicia's lifeless body falling to the ground, a ribbon of blood from her wounded skull, the only image in her mind's eye.

She did not know who screamed: herself, Mukai, the enforcers, the MAGI, or even the customers as they fled in panicked terror, but in the corner of her mind that could analyize, she knew the machine had taken over. In the end, when the blood and various off-plane ichors painted the still-repairing stage and floor, and the molecule-thin blades retracted into her uniform, Kate knew that the present scream belonged to her. Exploding grief and anguish and guilt echoed into a crescendo of pain…

…And then vanished.

The world was then replaced with the oddest –and most unpleasant– mix of sensations: a combination of severe vertigo and planar dysphoria: the result of shifting dimensions too rapidly. She retched into a prepared bucket, as a voice spoke soothing words to her. She felt something like a hand upon her back, holding her thick black hair away from her face as the contents of her stomach emptied in the backwash from the horrifying shock to her senses.

"There, there," the voice said. Through her sickness,

Kate realized by tone and accent that it was Dr. Galt who spoke to her, and that it was one of his pseudopods upon her back instead of his tiny, ugly hands. "The sickness is commonplace for what you went through. You passed, you know."

"Passed..?" Kate quavered in the midst of coughing after the nausea passed. She spat out the acidic remnants of bile and gingerly wiped her mouth with the back of her hand. A glass of water was presented to her, and she accepted it, taking small sips as to not set off the nausea again. "W … what happened? Where's Aly? Mukai? I was at Pink's … I think. I saw the MAGI …"

"You were sedated, and hooked to a VRSense network," the doctor said, letting go of Kate's hair as she struggled to sit up in the chair. "The mission, the betrayal: all of it was a simulation. All part of your psych exam."

The totality of everything that had happened, and the scope of the doctor's words at last registered. But strangely, she made little reaction to it. Her body still seemed to not accept it.

"So none of it happened?" Kate swallowed another sip of water that had suddenly gone tepid in her mouth. How'd you sedate…?" She froze with cold realization. "The tea!"

"I … ah … apologize for the deception, Lieutenant Barnes." His tone was shaky and mawkish and he began to stutter. It became clear to Kate that the Doctor was beginning to feel the full brunt of her emotions. "B-but we had to give you a s-s-simulation that you would accept … as completely real."

"You didn't have to do it the last time," Kate's voice came out distant and hollow as her initial shock receded and slowly gave way to burning rage. This was nothing else but a violation. The little four-armed creature had put her under and stuck her brain in a computer, running it through scenarios like a rat in a maze. Screw the purpose; this was akin to rape.

"W-we have t-to randomize the test for each p-p-participant, so that the r-results cannot be manip-manipulated by familiarity," the doctor attempted to explain in a voice that cracked like a squeaky wagon wheel. But by now, Kate was beyond either listening or caring. Her eyes downcast, she forced back the tirade that was building in her throat. "And you have to appreciate t-the ultimate harmlessness of ... of the whole ordeal."

Something inside Kate snapped.

"Harmless?" She shot out of the seat, and in one fluid bionic movement, slid forward and grabbed the doctor by the color of his bodysuit. She glared death into the beady green eyes that were set into the doctor's profusely sweating face. Baring her teeth as her biocomp rippled with weapons options and warnings, she noticed in her peripheral vision the dark patch that had begun to grow in the lower part of the doctor's uniform, as well as a sudden acrid acetone stench that grew in the air.

"You made me watch while one of my best friends killed my sister, you misshapen little kridball!" She stepped forward, and the doctor staggered backwards, his sweat exuding the pungent smell of acetone ever more. "Well, if you think that was harmless, then maybe you'll think this–" She narrowed the width of the heel on her foot padding, and stomped hard on a supporting pseudopod, "–is harmless!"

The doctor howled in pain. A black ichor from his wounded appendage stained the carpet as he collapsed against the wall behind him, exploding a string of expletives in his guttural native tongue. The biocomp offered a translation, and Kate declined as she stormed out of the lab. Several league techies gave her a wide berth when the exit door slid open.

The full force of her emotions came out much later, after the tedium of the calibration tests, when Kate at long last removed the uniform. It hurt like hell as it peeled off of her body in the shower stall, breaking some of her skin. Tiny rivulets of blood washed down the drain as she collapsed to the floor and huddled into a ball, her legs drawn against herself under the warm water's constant assault upon her raw skin. Truly alone now, away from the prying eyes of cameras and her uniform's biocomp, she cried.

Kate's true shame burned like a wound much deeper within. If it were weakness the doctor had been searching for, then he had indeed found it. Through all the implants and the near-invulnerable protection the uniform offered, an enforcer, the League's most elite defense force, was still a frail being in mind. Perhaps this was the reason that not a tear that Kate shed was from the pain that the nanomaterial had left behind.

THE END

Melody

"Come on Aly; it can't be that bad." Kate tried to be as reassuring as possible, but it seemed that her sister was, at this point, inconsolable. But it was understandable. After all, Alicia had known Kumai for years, whereas she and Alicia had only been reacquainted for less than a year, after learning that she had not been long dead as she had formerly thought.

Alicia, her long-lost sister had been the frontman for Ambush, the rock group she idolized in her teens and early twenties. Kate had been floored to learn that upon their reunion. She often figured that with all the time that had passed out-of-communication, she could hardly say that she still knew her sister now, especially seeing her so brokenhearted over this Gaen off-planer, Kumai, who had been her perpetual shadow, and now, noticeably, no longer there.

"How long has it been?" Kate asked. "I haven't been around much, you know."

"Three months." Alicia's skin seemed even paler, and that was truly something. It seemed to make the pronounced circles underneath her bleary, reddened eyes seem even more ghoulish. She picked half-heartedly at her marginally eaten steak, resting her chin heavily in her palm. "I'm surprised you hadn't noticed."

"Well, your house did seem a bit empty," Kate admitted with a halfhearted laugh, which she quickly suppressed upon Alicia's silence. "Damn. I knew I'd been kinda out of the loop, but … wow, *that* long?" Kate had inquired as to the whereabouts of the conspicuously absent, blue-skinned alien, and then Alicia had reacted with such an alarming gout of depression. "Wait. You *did* tell me that Kumai was like a housecat, right? That she just came and went as she pleased?"

"Yeah, but she's never been gone this long." Alicia said.

"No calls, no e-mail?"

Alicia's silence was answer enough.

"Hey, anyone ever told you that it's rude to put your elbows on the table?" Kate smiled, noting her sister's ungraceful posture, but her second weak attempt at levity was returned with only a vague twitch at the edge of Alicia's mouth.

"Wow, you really look like hell," Kate observed, "every bit the girl who lost her puppy."

"More like lost her kitty," Alicia murmured.

"Well, I see you *haven't* lost your sense of humor."

Kate frowned when Alicia gave no reaction. "Look, she's come back before, right? So maybe she'll come back again."

"She left a note this time," Alicia said, and reached into her pants pocket. She removed a neatly folded note on stationary with her band's stylized "A" extended into music bars, at the top. Kate received the paper and read over the hastily scrawled words, written with obvious difficulty by a hand that was more used to the fluid calligraphy of the *Glossiu* alphabet of Gaea.

"She said that she hadn't been feeling close to me," Alicia said as Kate scanned over the letter, written in the too-perfect cursive of someone who had used a nerve interface for writing English words that by herself would have been too difficult for lack of practice. She watched her sister shove a piece of steak into her mouth, and then chew it mechanically, it as if out of duty or chore rather than pleasure. "She said that I was never around enough, and that she was tired of travelling from one world to the next with me giving no attention to her. She needed time to herself to 'consider our relationship.' She seemed pretty pissed about it too. Hell, I didn't even think we *had* a relationship! At least she was considerate enough to hand the reins of management to Stacie before I left. She was the only member of the managing staff who I could trust worth a damn."

"Well, Gaeans *do* have a reputation for being just about the most unadventurous of any off-planers," Kate said, handing the paper back to Alicia, folded just as carefully as before. "If it weren't for the League's advantages, I don't think that they would bother much with Earth. They're homebodies, especially Kumai's gender. Alpha females are pretty much geared towards home and family. The letter says it all. Simply put, she missed you. You weren't giving her any attention. Their mates mean a great deal to them, you know."

Alicia's eyes widened as her hand paused with the fork halfway to her mouth. "Wait a minute," Her voice was an almost sepulchral dead monotone. "Rewind just a bit. What do you mean, 'mate'?"

Kate's brows furrowed. "She called you tir-Alicia, didn't she? I heard it all the time when she talked to you."

"Well, yeah," Alicia drawled out, as if the question were about something that was as common as the sky being blue, "but I thought it was just some Gaean term of endearment, or that she was saying "dear Alicia," and just couldn't pronounce the 'D' right." It sounded to me like she was saying 'teer-Ah-*lee*-see-ah' all the time." She repeated the words in rapid succession, mimicking Kumai's high soprano and almost-staccatto accent. A weak half-smile crept upon her lips and a wistful look came to her eyes. "It was kind of annoying, actually, like how Mukai calls you *saatu-Kate* all the time."

"*Saatu* means 'friend,'" Kate pointedly remarked. "*Tir* … well, it has many meanings: 'companion,' 'partner,' 'lover'…" Quickly shaking her head, she corrected herself. "Wait, no, not 'lover.' Really, the closest word is 'mate'."

Alicia leaned forward, a fire lit in her eyes that had not been there before. "Are you fucking *serious*?" Her voice cracked like an adolescent singer as her eyes locked upon her sister with full incredulity.

"Yeah," Kate said matter-of-factly. "That's what Gaeans call someone whom they've bonded with. You didn't know?"

Alicia looked away, abashed, her lips pursed in restrained shame.

"I can see now why Kumai left."

"What's that supposed to mean?" Alicia fired off testily. Kate's question had supplanted her depression by a new, dangerous spark in her eyes.

"What I mean," Kate replied, placid, despite Alicia's outburst, "is that it looks like that you never bothered to learn about Gaeans during the time that Kumai was hanging around you. Tell me, how much did you really know about Kumai's past? Did you ever bother to ask her? How much Glossiu do you know? Did you ever ask her to teach you, or even go out and buy a translation matrix so you could learn it? What's Kumai's favorite food? What does she-?"

"All right, all right! Alicia snapped, emphatically waving for Kate to stop. "I get you, okay? Look, Kumai just kind of popped into my life, you know? She did it all at once, and so comfortably, that it was like I'd always known her, even though I didn't. We just … well, I guess we just clicked; I don't know how else to say it. I didn't bother to think much deeper into how or why. She just fit with me; she felt right. At the time, I was too hopped up on circus to really care about why she hung around me … and then after I cleaned up and we got the band back together, I was just so busy all the time. And now you're telling me she saw me as a mate? Like a wife or something?"

"Yeah, pretty much." For the first time in several minutes, Kate paused to take a draft from her half-finished mug of beer. "I'm guessing you didn't quite see her that way?"

"I didn't know *what* to see her as," Alicia confessed. "She just 'walked in' one day and stayed. I was on Gaea for a stopover the night before Rax got arrested and everything went to hell. She and I got to talking at this little dive in Mezedia; next thing I know, she's coming home with me. I just let her. She followed me around like a lost puppy after that, but I didn't seem to mind, even on days when I was sober. I don't know why I didn't. God, I had a boyfriend once; Walker was a great guy. We were pretty serious until he was killed. Krid, we fucked like bunnies the first few months. I was never into women-"

"Kumai's not a woman," Kate warned.

"Right, right," Alicia said, annoyed at the interruption. "But she damn sure looks like a woman, at least at first glance. And yes, I learned pretty quickly that she wasn't. Hell, she never started calling me 'tir-Alicia' until the first time that we…" She bit her lip, and stopped, a slight nod conveying the fact that she entrusted the rest to imagination.

"Now you know why she calls you that,'" Kate said. You are her mate, as far as she's concerned, *and* as far as her people are concerned. Relationships, especially intimate ones, aren't just a 'hit it and quit it' thing to Gaeans. They take them very seriously."

Alicia was dead silent for several minutes, picking at her steak once again, as if checking it for vermin, her expression rolling disturbingly back and forth between confusion and pain. Finally, she steeled herself, and took a deep breath.

"Okay, then, Katie. Let's suppose I accept Kumai's being my 'mate'. I'm thinking you know more about Gaeans than I do?"

"A lot more." Kate tried without success to hide the hint of smugness that crept into her voice.

"Well, what's your take on all this? Just why have I been so comfortable with Kumai around? And why does it hurt so much that she's gone? I mean, I admit that I cared about the blueberry, but I never felt like there was anything really strong between us when she was around. Why is it that she's been all I can think about for the past few days, to the point where I can't write any music. If for nothing else, then do it for the band. We're starting to suffer because of it."

"Okay, then..." Kate boosted herself upright in her chair. She pressed her hands together after making a dramatic show of working the kinks out of her neck muscles. "Gaean gender relations 101: alpha females and you." She paused, eyeing with amusement the tenaciously unamused expression on her sister's face. "You see, alpha females like Kumai find their mates by chemistry. I mean literal chemistry. Pheremones, or something; even Gaeans aren't sure what it is, exactly. Short story is, once she finds someone she 'likes,' she sticks with that person for life. Weirdly enough, that person tends to stay with her as well." She gulped down another long draft of her beer, finishing it off. "I've just never heard of it happening to a human. Hell, I doubt

111

any scientists, human or Gaean have heard of it. Most humans are …" she pursed her lips, finding no way to make her choice of words easy, "… put off by Gaeans, I guess. They find them too creepy. You don't seem to mind them, though; hell, neither do I. Mukai's my closest off-planer friend. But I'd never date a Gaean myself. Your relationship with Kumai must be one for the record books."

"I'm not a freak, sis," Alicia said in a slightly hurt tone, but then conceded a little after a moment of thought. "But … I guess I am a little weird."

"Aren't we all?" Kate's quip elicited a mutual guffaw between the two sisters before she continued. "Long separation between mates when it comes to alpha females can be painful, from what I've heard. Depression sets in; they usually get over it, but there have been a few cases of suicide."

"Aww, great." Alicia planted her face in her hands, her falls of straight black hair with purple highlights forming a mop around the shape of her head. Her long, drawn-out groan was muffled by her palm. "Krid… just perfect. So now I'm tethered to this blue-skinned housecat under pain of suicide? Is that what you're saying?"

Kate eyed her sister incredulously. "No, that's not what I'm saying. And wait just a minute; is Kumai that much of a problem for you? What happened to all that stuff about you two getting along so well, and how you just clicked? Don't you care about her at all?"

"I…!"

All protests instantly died upon Alicia's lips as Kate's words sunk in. Their truth rang with a reverb that reduced her pride to powder. When she spoke again, her tone was much more subdued and contrite.

"Well, I…I don't *not* care for her."

"That's more like it," Kate said. "From what you've been telling me, it looks like you've at least accepted her. Besides, it's not like you're the only human who's hooked up with an off-planer. Bond or no bond, it's only natural that after five months, you'd start to miss her. At the very least, you two were friends."

"Well, based on what you said, if I'm starting to feel this way, then that means that Kumai is feeling this way too," Alicia proposed. "Am I right?"

"Not necessarily."

Alicia was crestfallen. "What do you mean, 'not necessarily'?"

"I never said it happens at the same time."

"You know, you're not making this easier for me, sis." Even more depressed than before, Alicia made a halfhearted attempt at wiping the stray strands of hair from her face. Instead of moving her hand back to the table, she brought it back to her forehead, allowing her hair to fall back into its encircling purple and black mop about her head. "Damn… I never thought I'd miss her so much! It hurts so bad, Katie. It really hurts! And the band's been working on a new album, and I can't do krid for them, and it's been pissing them off. This is hell."

Alicia's voice, already quavering with her last couple

of sentences, at last broke into a full despairing, wailing, heartbroken sob. "Dammit, blueberry! Dammit! Why did you have to leave me?"

Saying nothing, Kate stood up from her side of the table, and then knelt beside Alicia. She needed no words, and only held her sister as she cried, keening over the loss of someone whom she had completely taken for granted. She could only imagine how hard this was for her.

"Look, Aly, I think I've got an idea," Kate said as her sister's sobs began to soften. The words came hesitant and uncertain, as she was unsure if it was appropriate to speak. She paused, and Alicia's crying had faded to silence, although she kept her face buried in her hands. Satisfied that she was not at least being ignored, Kate continued. "Why don't I check with Jackie, and see if we can find out where Kumai is, exactly? It'd be a slight abuse of power as an enforcer, but I'm sure we can locate her."

"You'd do that?" Alicia's voice came out as wet as her cheeks as she wiped away the still profuse tears from her reddened eyes.

Kate fixed Alicia with a wry grin. "I'm your sister. It's my duty … in addition to bugging the hell out of you."

Alicia shook with another lazy guffaw, one eye glancing her sister's way with another smile that suited her much better than misery. "Okay then. It's better than nothing, I guess. Thanks, Katie. And yeah, I'd like that very much."

Alicia then reached down and rolled up the hem of her black denim jeans to reveal grungy, military-style boots that were scuffed and worn with age. She reached into the lip and removed a folded piece of paper from a secret compartment sewn into the fabric. She handed it to Kate.

Kate unfolded the paper to reveal an old photo. It had been printed out on plain copier paper, rather than glossy photo paper, and so the image showed little damage aside from the multiple creases. In the photo, both Alicia and Kumai were seated at a table, the background reminiscent of Pink's, the restaurant on the old transcontinental bridge that Alicia now owned and where she held concerts from time to time. Alicia was leaning on Kumai's shoulder, one arm draped lazily around the off-planer's neck, the other holding a mug of beer that was about the size of her head. Alicia's dark sunglasses concealed eyes that were most likely bloodshot, and there was an odd flush to Kumai's face. Both of them were grinning from ear to ear, presumably from a great deal of alcohol that had been imbibed. Kumai's immaculately white teeth showed dramatically against the blue of her skin.

"I know you can search video records," Alicia said, "but I'm hoping that pic will give the computers something to match up with and speed up your search."

"It's recent?" Kate asked, standing up and re-folding the photo. Carefully, she slipped it into the back pocket of her jeans.

"Pretty recent. It was the last picture we took before

she left, at a wrap-up party for one of our tours. It was about a year ago, I think. I hope she hasn't changed much."

"I doubt she has," Kate said, reaching for her leather jacket that had been slung over the back of the chair. "Look, I'm going to swing on by League HQ and have Jackie begin a search."

"Can't you just eye fax it to her?" Alicia gestured towards Kate's eyes, much sharper in their angles than her own, giving her sister's face a sharper, almost predatory edge, except when she smiled. I know you enforcers can do that."

Kate shook her head. "Not when the director might see it. He checks to see if we even sneeze wrong. Too many damn regulations. It's best that I take it directly to Jackie. She knows ways around security."

Look, sis, this ..." Alicia halted in her speech, sounding almost awkward in saying the words. "This really means a lot to me. If you find her, could you tell her how sorry I am? I miss her like crazy."

The two sisters made their way through a hallway that connected the dining room to the front foyer, where Alicia's gold and platinum records lined the white sheetrock walls between intermittent potted plants. Kate, having slipped into her jacket, pulled her younger sister into a hug. "You don't have to thank me. I knew she meant a lot to you since I first met her, even though you didn't seem to realize it." Releasing the embrace, she smiled at the hopeful tears that flowed down Alicia's cheeks, distorting the tiny star-shaped tattoo beneath her left eye to where it looked twice its normal size. "And I'll tell her what you said. But I think that you need to tell her that when you see her again."

"We'll have a lot of things to talk about," Alicia said, swallowing back more tears as Kate reached for the door. No sooner had her fingers touched its gold plated knob, however, than the doorbell rang: its familiar eight tone church-like chimes echoing throughout the house as Kate pulled the door fully open.

Kate staggered back at the sight of the visitor, unwittingly blocking Alicia's view. For several seconds, silence hung like a sword of Damocles in the middle of the foyer.

"Um … found her," Kate said at last, sounding like a precocious schoolgirl who had easily discovered the answer to a complicated math problem.

"Found who?" Alicia stepped forward slowly at first, and then like Kate, staggered back unbelieving at the sight that greeted her eyes.

"Kumai…?"

Alicia stood, slack jawed for about three seconds at the statuesque off-planer who stood on the porch … and then she bounded towards the doorway, nearly shoving Kate aside. Grasping hard at the door post with one hand, she roughly wiped away the remaining tears that clung to her eyes with the other, dispelling the blurriness of her vision, her face a mask of astonished delight, and barely contained joy.

Kumai had not changed one bit. Her hair was the same: long, straight, immaculately styled in beautiful falls and intricate braids, and pure silvery white. She had not changed what few cosmetics she wore upon her medium-blue skin, and her eggshell white clothes still resembled that fusion of business casual and evening wear that Gaeans had a knack for. A smile graced her glossed blue lips, and tiny twin streams of tears began to trickle down her cheeks, leaving transparent trails from her liquid black eyes.

"Tir-Alicia…" Kumai's incongruously high-pitched voice quavered as her hand slowly lowered from the doorbell. She raised her opposite hand with the same speed as Alicia reached out for her. Both of them were hesitant, until Kumai's blue digits came into contact with Alicia's ashen fingertips.

"You're real." Alicia swallowed, biting her lower lip as new tears fell. Her voice cracked and quavered. "God… it's not a dream!"

Kumai nodded: a gesture that was vague and almost imperceptible. "Kumai has come back to you, tir-Alicia."

Alicia wasted no more words, and completed the distance between them in no time, nearly falling into Kumai's embrace, the word "blueberry" escaping her lips in an elated, husky whisper. The silence of the grand house and of the night was broken afterwards only by their shuddering breaths and sniffles amidst their reunion. Quietly, Kate slipped past them and down the walkway back to the street where she had parked her motorcycle. She smiled, and spoke under her breath as she moved silently beneath the boughs of lifelike holographic oaks, kept out of reach by the house's high irongate.

"Yep, sis, I'd say that you far more than just accepted her."

****

The curtains were drawn, expunging all traces of light from the bedroom, save the subdued glow of sparse lamplight. In truth, Alicia did not care about what time it was. Neither she, nor Kumai, she believed, had thought about time since their torrent of emotions had boiled over in their tearful reunion and they had made it to the bed.

Time coupled with air conditioning had evaporated the sheen of sweat from the Gaean's soft, blue skin, but it still emitted a delicate, sweet scent that reminded Alicia of roses. She smiled, inhaling deeply as she rested her head upon Kumai's lap, both their bodies partially exposed and concealed by disheveled bed sheets and discarded clothing, carelessly strewn about. With this sparse covering, it was plain to see how Kumai's slightly elongated abdomen contributed to the height difference between herself and Alicia. Though slender and curvaceous as any human female, Kumai's not-quite-human body proportions made her noticeably taller than most, and easily a full head taller than Alicia was. Her abdominal muscles were also more clearly defined than human women, giving her belly an almost masculine appearance, with two navels instead of one. Her body was also completely hairless, save her eyebrows and head, and her breasts were very small in comparison to her height: barely A-cups if at all that large, Alicia supposed, though, she had been quick to discover, much to her amusement and delight, that they were disproportionately sensitive for their size.

"God, I missed this!" Alicia heaved a sigh of complete contentment, her words coming out in an almost drunken drawl. She moved her head back and forth upon Kumai's soft thighs as she released the stress that was bound in her shoulder and neck muscles. Kumai looked on with a soft, mildly amused expression.

"Kumai has missed this as well. Kumai's lap has felt lonely these past five months."

Kumai had spoken little since she arrived —not that words would have been of any use in expressing themselves during the past couple of hours. Alicia saw the gentle smile upon Kumai's soft lips ... felt Kumai run her fingers softly through her shoulder-length midnight black hair, the polar opposite in color to the off-planer's snowy cascade. With both of their crowning glories hopelessly disheveled, Alicia giggled at the futile attempt that was being made to straighten hers out.

"You know, fingers don't work as well as combs, blueberry," Alicia remarked, "but I appreciate the effort."

"Kumai misses this too," Kumai said, her voice serene and quiet. "Kumai missed you so much, tir-Alicia."

"You've been saying that a lot," Alicia observed, recalling with amusement how that phrase had been just about the only thing that Kumai had been able to say throughout the night. "I think we spent the last hour or two re-familiarizing ourselves with things we missed."

Kumai's low, melodious laugh was like the strings of a harp.

And it looks like we at least got rid of stress that we don't miss," Alicia added, and then took note of the ensuing palpable silence between them. It took a moment, but despite the fact that Kumai's liquid black eyes revealed nothing of her thoughts, it at last dawned upon Alicia that she had been waiting for something. Alicia had always found it difficult to read the mysterious Gaean who had made herself such an indelible fixture in her life, but this time, her desire was all too clear.

"I missed you too, Kumai."

Alicia discovered, much to her initial surprise, that she did not need to bring conviction into her voice when she made this confession. Her heart split open at the words, and once again, she felt the wetness of tears flow from her eyes and onto Kumai's lap. She reached for a section of the bed sheet and dabbed away at her face and Kumai's skin. "More than you know."

Alicia felt Kumai's hand move from her hair to her loosely open right hand. Reflexively her fingers curled upon it, and she felt more at peace than ever, even after the long interlude of intimacy that they had shared. Alicia had never quite understood their relationship, and despite how far she had allowed it to go, constantly questioned what Kumai had meant to her, or what she meant to Kumai. Kumai, however, seemed perfectly content to be with her from the night she followed her home. She had asked for nothing, and gave her everything, remaining a steadfast companion, even agreeing to become Ambush's manager even after Alicia had nearly self-destructed on circus and was brought to the brink of death. When they first shared their bed, she had passed it off as satisfying blind curiosity, but soon came to realize after more nights together that sex with Kumai did not feel at all strange. In fact, she felt just as comfortable with Kumai, just as complete as she had felt with Walker, all those many years ago. And the two of them had been the closest of friends and steadfast lovers.

"What are you thinking about, tir-Alicia?" Kumai asked, taking note of her silence.

"A lot of things."

"Like …?"

"Well, for starters, where were you for the past three months?"

"Home." Kumai had said this after a suspiciously long pause. "Kumai had tried to start anew, but the pain became too great."

The pain of that separation, which had quickly become all but a distant memory, elicited a vague shudder in Alicia's body. "On Gaea, then? But where at home were you? And what were you doing?"

"Teaching."

Again, there was that pause, with a single answer that explained little. Alicia felt slight frustration rise within her. "You're being kinda vague, blueberry."

"It was … a difficult time for Kumai," Kumai said, still obviously, irritatingly, secretive. But when she spoke, it was with a finality that was uncharacteristic for her. "It is…difficult to talk about. When Kumai is ready, then Kumai will tell you."

Alicia sulked for a moment. It was not like Kumai to be so evasive, and that caused a tinge of worry to darken the moment. But she did not want to push the issue, especially when it was obvious that Kumai did not want to talk about it. She quickly decided that she would not let it ruin her mood, and cast her frustrations from her mind.

"Oh, all right, then; keep your little secrets." With a sigh, Alicia sat up and faced Kumai, propping herself on splayed palms. She looked the Gaean directly in the fathomless depths of her black-within-black eyes: something she had never been able to do before.

"You know, I was thinking about one other thing. Hell, it's something that has been going through my mind ever since you came into my life, but I never could quite get the courage to ask. Maybe it was because I had just decided to accept it, but … well …"

She closed her eyes, steeling her courage against Kumai's soul-piercing stare.

"Kumai, what did you see in me that night we first met? And why did you choose me? Why not a Gaean beta female … a … what did you call them? *Kalampu*?

They're at least used to these kinds of relationships. Or what about a male? A *kelempra*?" Alicia felt a surge of pride at knowing at least that little bit of the language. "Just what am I to you?"

Alicia felt Kumai's gentle touch upon her right shoulder. She closed her eyes and bit her lip as goosebumps erupted upon the synthetic skin of her artificial arm.

"You chose Kumai."

Recovering from the pleasant sensation that Kumai had induced, Alicia made a tiny guffaw. "I think it's the other way, blueberry. *You're* the one who followed *me* home, after all."

Kumai shook her head, her smile beatific. "No, tir-Alicia. *You* chose *Kumai*. Kumai is *kalampra*. *Kalampu* and *Kelempra* choose us. They ..." She frowned, thinking of the right words to say. "At a point in life, one of both ... calls to us when we see them, and we follow. You called to Kumai. Kumai followed."

Alicia's mind went blank for a moment. Unable to make sense of what Kumai had just said, she was unsure of what to say about this until she remembered that Kate had mentioned how even Gaeans themselves were unsure about how the bond with alpha females worked. So perhaps it made sense for this explanation to not make sense. The only thing clear about what Kumai had said was that she was most certainly, irrevocably bonded to her. So like it or not, when she went to that bar on that fateful night, she had inadvertently picked up a sort of take-home spouse.

But of course, it had not been a bad thing.

"What about my other question?" Alicia asked with a casualness that belied her inability to comprehend Kumai's explanation.

To this, Kumai's long, slender fingers traced their way to Alicia's cheek, and then to her lips. Alicia suppressed a smile, but could not help feeling the hairs on the back of her neck stand on end.

"You are everything to Kumai. You are tir-Alicia."

Alicia sat upright, and Kumai leaned forward, sliding her arms around Alicia's neck. Alicia inhaled and again detected the rose-like scent. It was quite strong upon her skin. Another thing that Alicia noticed, were the tears that had appeared upon Kumai's face.

"But tir-Alicia, Kumai must ask you … how can Kumai not yet be tir-Kumai to you? The off-planer's high-pitched voice shook and quavered amidst shuddering breaths. "Tir-Alicia, Kumai has told you what you are to Kumai. But … what is *Kumai* to *you*?"

Kumai's words squeezed hard at Alicia's heart like a pair of industrial pliers. The distress of the Gaean's voice and the tears were enough to remind her of the conversation with Kate over how one-sided this relationship had been, as well as what relationship it truly was. It was now impossible to deny the depth of the feelings she had for this off-planer who had wandered unbidden into her life like a housecat, but gave her all of herself, body and soul. Alicia had accepted it without question, and found Kumai remarkably easy to talk to, work with …

… and even love.

Despite her initially conflicted emotions, she now saw Kumai as a true partner. Unusual though the circumstances of their first meeting had been, she and Kumai were indeed mates: companions in life, bound together, body and soul, for better or worse. At long last, she had come to accept it. No, she *welcomed* it.

"You *are* tir-Kumai."

Alicia had expected the words to sound alien and wrong, but it was just the opposite. They felt just as right, just as perfect as when she had spoken words of love to Walker in the bedroom all those many years ago.

"You're everything to me as well, blueberry," Alicia reached out to wipe the tears away from Kumai's eyes, still widened in shock over her confession. "I'm so sorry it took such a long time to admit that. And I'm sorry for taking you for granted like I had. Hell, when I almost burnt my brain out on circus and destroyed the nerves in my arm, you stood by me when I had no one. You were there for me when I was just some nameless has-been. And even then, I was a real bitch to you. I really don't deserve you." Once again, she looked Kumai directly in her fathomless eyes. "I'm so sorry, Kumai. I'll never hurt you like I did, ever again. I promise. You're a part of me now. We belong to each other."

"Tir-Alicia…" Kumai's white teeth shone blindingly against the blue background of her face.

Alicia caressed Kumai's flushed cheek, her thumb passing softly over her lips. "Tir-Kumai…" She whispered. "Tell me, how do you say, 'I love you' in

Glossiu?"

"*Mel'idii*," Kumai said, and her smile grew.

"*Mel'idii*." Alicia repeated it several times, mastering the pronunciation with her mouth and savoring the feeling that its meaning produced within her heart.

"*Mel'idii*, tir-Kumai."

With a touch of lips and then blue skin to pale tan, an explosion of rose scent, and a burst of renewed vigor, human and Gaean lost count of the hours once again, and love healed the raw, throbbing scars caused by years of callousness and neglect, and the separation of five months.

****

Kate was impressed. She had returned from the restroom to find the very last thing she would expect: Mukai and Alicia holding a conversation in perfect Glossiu. Though her sister's dialect was noticeably different, Mukai, who knew very little Earth English without the aid of the translation matrix for her INplant, did not seem to have any problems understanding her. Kate, however, found it somewhat difficult to comprehend some of the words and idioms that Alicia was using.

"…And you know, it is weird, but Kumai's breasts have actually gotten bigger. It's the strangest thing! Is that normal for *kalampra*?" Alicia was saying.

To this, Mukai pursed her dark blue lips thoughtfully.

"It would not be strange at all, friend Alicia, if she-"

"Well, this is new!" Breaking into the conversation, Kate sat down beside Mukai, who seemed just as pleasantly surprised as she was. Mukai, unlike Kumai, was a beta female – a "true" female of her species, and therefore was much shorter and better endowed than any alpha female. "You've been holding out on me, sis. When did you get so good at speaking Glossiu?"

"Tir-Kumai has been teaching Alicia like mad," Alicia replied in Glossiu. "And it helps to have a T-matrix to speed things up. But most of it Alicia learned without help."

Kate stared at first, her eyes wide. Then she sputtered, and then burst out with a belly laugh that attracted nearly every last bit of attention from nearby restaurant guests.

"Come on! It's not that funny!" Alicia had switched back to English. "It's not my fault that Kumai's dialect doesn't use singular first-person personal pronouns."

"I'm sorry." Kate swallowed back the rest of her conniption fit, wiping away at her teary eyes with the palm of her hand. "Really, sis. I am. I can understand Kumai referring to herself in the third person, but it just sounds so gosh-darn cute coming from you!" She turned to Mukai, who had become somewhat self-conscious after having received so many stares, and switched to Glossiu. "Hey, Mukai, would Kumai understand you if you referred to yourself in the first person?"

"Of course, friend Kate," Mukai nodded cordially. "Our dialects are mutually intelligible." She turned to

Alicia, speaking in her halting English. "Would you … like to … learn it … *saatu*-Alicia?"

"God, yes," Alicia's voice lilted with relief. "It's so clumsy and embarrassing, talking that way."

Mukai's laugh was soft and genteel like Kumai's, almost a titter, but in a tone that was of much lower pitch. "I have not heard of it described that way," she said, switching back to Glossiu, "but I think you are the first human to learn that dialect; mine is considered standard. But I will teach you."

It took no time for Alicia to master the word, and she heartily thanked Mukai for the lesson. When she switched to Glossiu, she now spoke it with less trepidation, slipping the pronoun easily into her sentences, rather than pausing abashed at having to use her own name repeatedly.

"We speak Glossiu most of the time now," Alicia said. "We made a lot of mutual promises. She's gone back to managing the band, and I'm trying to be a better friend to her than I've been before."

"Just a friend?" Kate said.

"At the most basic level." Alicia could not help but reveal a grin.

Kate nodded approvingly. "I'd say you're doing a good job of it. Kumai seemed much happier than before, last time I came by."

"Yeah, I should've done this a long time ago. It feels like we're making up for lost time."

"In that and other things," Kate remarked with a wry grin. "It's been damn hard to get you at home, especially in the evening."

"Friend Kate!" Mukai ejected reproachfully, but Alicia had tipped her hand with a simple deep blush.

"Well, you don't hear her complaining," Kate observed in a playful tone. She gestured casually towards her sister. "Why I'd say that she and Kumai have…"

With distracting suddenness, a strange sound erupted from Alicia, like grunt mixed with a repressed strain. The noise stopped Kate mid-tease as she shifted her gaze. The redness of Alicia's face had suddenly turned alarmingly green.

"Friend Alicia…?" Mukai stiffened and leaned forward as Alicia's eyes bulged and her cheeks puffed out slightly. Alicia slapped her hand over her mouth, and then with silent urgency, nearly kicked the chair into the table behind her as she bolted towards the restroom.

"Sis!" Kate stood bolt upright, watching with the rest of the confused guests as Alicia disappeared into the restroom alcove. "Wait here, Mukai," Kate said with unintentional terseness as she briskly made her own way to the restroom, trying hard not to change her brisk pace into a flat-out run. Kate paused at the door, the sound coming from inside nauseatingly familiar. The door was locked, and she pressed against its metal surface.

"Alicia, you okay? You need me to call an ambulance?"

Kate heard her sister retch a second, third, and fourth

time, followed by silence that increased her distress.

"Aly? You alive in there?"

Kate had been about to start the emergency dialing sequence on her biocomp when there came the sound of a toilet flushing. Alicia's voice followed, much to her relief, but it sounded weak and shaky.

"I'm all right, Katie. You ..." there was an odd pause. "You don't need to call an ambulance, 'kay?"

A moment later, there came the sound of water running followed by the subdued roar of a hand dryer. The door opened and Alicia staggered through, looking almost as drained as the night she had been crying about Kumai's three-month absence. Groaning, she held her hand gingerly to her stomach.

"Geez, Aly!" Kate shrank back at her sister's appearance. "You look like you ate the chili. And we haven't even eaten yet."

"I feel worse," Alicia grimaced and Kate draped her arm around her shoulder, steadying her as they made their way back to the table. "I really don't need this. We've got a tour lined up in about a week. Kumai had to pull some major strings for our locations, too."

"Wait a minute." Kate stopped, mid-stride, nearly bumping into a robot waiter. "How long has this been going on?"

"About a week now, I think," Alicia said. "Look, let's get back to the table before we talk more. I'm feeling kinda dizzy here."

"Sure, sis." Kate brought her sister back to the table, where Mukai waited, concern having melted into relief upon her face.

"You are feeling better, friend Alicia?" She asked.

"Yeah. A little." Alicia rubbed the bridge of her nose as she leaned forward. Almost out of habit from Kumai's rigorous training, she slipped into Glossiu. "At least the dizziness is gone. But it's been hard for me to hold meals down lately."

"Hey, you might be pregnant!" Kate quickly regretted her joke, however, at the sight of Alicia's withering glare.

"Not funny," her sister growled icily.

"Sorry, I was just trying to cheer you up," Kate said contritely. "I'm really worried for you, you know. You said you've been feeling like this for about a week?"

"Yeah. It came on pretty sudden. It hasn't gotten worse or anything, but I haven't been able to hold anything down in the morning. And I've been feeling like krid all day. Eating hasn't been very pleasant either."

Kate was appalled. "And you haven't gone to see a doctor yet?"

"I was planning on doing it this Monday," Alicia protested. "I was just worried that it was something serious."

"That's more reason than ever to find out," Kate said. "In the case of your health, ignorance isn't bliss, you know."

"Friend Alicia..."

Mukai had been oddly silent for the last few moments, lost in thought from what Kate could see.

But now, there was a strange look on the Gaean's face that neither sister could comprehend. "How long has it been since cestoia?"

"Excuse me?" Alicia paused at the unfamiliar Glossiu word before her T-matrix kicked in. A strange expression then crossed her face, albeit a different one from Mukai's. "My ... period?"

Mukai nodded, her expression even less readable than usual.

"Um..." Alicia flustered for a moment, eyeing Mukai strangely. Her voice lowered into a whisper when she spoke again. "Why the hell would you want to know that?"

"How long?" Mukai said, undaunted.

"Mukai, Kate was just teasing me. I'm pretty sure it's-"

"How long?"

Though secretly alarmed at Mukai's resolute sternness, Alicia sighed with feigned annoyance and began to do a mental calculation on her fingertips. A moment later, her brow furrowed in confusion, and she hurriedly went through the math again, and then a third time. Each time, her expression darkened just a bit more.

"Aly...?" Kate touched Alicia's hand, mid count.

"Damn, that just can't be right," Alicia said, more to herself than anyone else.

"*What* can't be right?" Kate asked.

Alicia's hands fell to the tabletop; her gaze seemed far away, as if rejecting reality.

"I'm late."

****

"I really hate this, Katie."

"You've said that about fifty times now." Kate checked her watch for what seemed like the fiftieth time while Alicia fidgeted on the examination table, fiddling uselessly with the ever-loosening seams of the revealing back of her lime green hospital gown.

"You didn't even let me eat!"

"Would you have been able to hold down the food?"

Alicia opened her mouth, and then swallowed her words, knowing that she had been on the verge of dry heaving right before they left the restaurant. Kate had to cancel their order and leave Mukai to eat by herself as she scheduled a same-day appointment at the League clinic, much to Alicia's initial chagrin. She had complained that she had money to go see other physicians, but Kate insisted, stating, in addition to League HQ being closer than any hospital, that health care for family members of League personnel was free.

"I'm bored as hell."

"You didn't look too bored when several of the nurses came in wanting your autograph," Kate said smugly.

"That was an hour ago," Alicia said in her defense. "I guess the place doesn't get too many celebrities."

"Not many." Kate gave a soft laugh. "And it was an hour and a half ago, actually."

"Whatever!" Alicia's burst of anger startled Kate, but it abated quickly. Alicia frowned, puffing out a loud exhale. "Look, I'm sorry, sis. It's just that … well … I'm a little bit on edge here. I don't know what the hell to make of all this. I mean, what does Mukai know about humans? You can't really think that she was right …" She paused, waiting for a response that never came. "… Can you?"

"I trust Mukai," Kate said. "She thinks there might be something to this; I don't know what, but that's what we're here to find out."

"She didn't even explain her hunch," Alicia glared distantly at the examination's room's exit door, "only said it was 'personal,' if what she thought was true. What the hell does that mean anyway?"

"That's Gaeans for you," Kate said with a shrug. "I'm kinda wondering that myself, but the detective in me needs more information. You know, Gaeans aren't all that different from humans when it comes to reproduction. With the exception of needing a third gender for it, pretty much everything else is the same. I'm pretty sure Mukai knew this."

"Yeah, but alphas aren't supposed to be able to make a person pregnant," Alicia said, and then shook her head. "Why am I even entertaining this? I'm not pregnant! That's impossible!"

"Perhaps," Kate said, "but I bet that there's probably more to it than that. I'm sure we'll understand when the doctor comes back."

"Yeah … the doctor …" Alicia curled her legs up to

her chest on the exam table, and said nothing more. An indeterminable time passed between the two sisters: one tense and worried, the other cautious and calculating in the silence of the examination room. Kate had opened up the I-Link port on her wrist and had been checking her e-mail when Alicia chose to speak again, her question coming out in a whisper that Kate had almost not detected.

"Sis…?"

"Mm?" Kate looked up from the hologram and switched it off.

"I'm scared. What if it's something serious?"

"No." Kate hoisted herself up onto the table, setting herself beside Alicia. She draped her arm over her sister's shoulder. "Don't think like that. You're going to be all right, okay?"

Alicia sniffled loudly and wetly, and then nodded, resting her head upon Kate's shoulder.

"I wish we'd told Kumai about this."

"You didn't want me to," Kate reminded her. "Remember? You said that there was no need to worry her."

"Oh." Alicia inhaled deeply, and then sighed. "Guess I'm just having second thoughts."

"Well, it's a little too late for that now," Kate said.

As if Kate's words had been portentous, the door opened. The doctor stepped through, the form-fitting medical suit upon his bark-like skin resembling Kate's enforcer uniform, but white instead of black, and more angular and masculine where hers sported sleek curves. A red medical cross was emblazoned upon its right breast while, as it did on Kate's uniform, the half star symbol of the League graced the left. The long, flat, leaf-like appendages that composed what passed for his "hair" twitched and undulated as he glanced at the digital records upon the hologram at his wrist with multifaceted eyes.

"Well, the test results are in." The doctor's mouth formed the words, but the pleasant, human-like sound of his voice originated from his fronds of leaf-hair. "You can breathe easy, Ms. Barnes. It's nothing serious. In fact, it's good news. You're pregnant."

A pin drop would have sounded like thunder. And Alicia's single whispered word was like an explosion.

"No..."

Kate's expression had been that of concern and concentration, but Alicia was broken. She was shaking her head when she spoke, and trembling. Tears began to stream profusely from her eyes.

"No, no, no, no!" Alicia shook her head harder, grimacing as Kate tried to put her arm around her shoulder once again. Alicia forcefully shrugged it off. "No way! No way in hell!"

"Oh." The doctor's expression had changed quickly to concern. "I ... gather this was unplanned?"

"No, you don't understand!" Alicia jumped off of the examination table and began to pace frantically across the floor. "She's a Gaean! She's an alpha, not even male or female. We've been together for over two years; I've lost count of the times we had sex; none of it was protected; there was nothing to be protected from! She can't get me pregnant! It should be impossible!"

"A ... Gaean?" the doctor said, nonplussed.

"Yes, am I mumbling or something?" Alicia spat, no longer bothering to control herself. "So you tell me, doc: how the hell could this have happened? Either you screwed up the prognosis, or your equipment is infected with a bad case of bullkrid!"

"Aly, calm down!" Kate jumped down from the examination table and grabbed her sister by the wrists before she begin whaling on the stunned and terrified doctor. "You're making a scene."

Her sister's touch brought Alicia back to reality. Hot anger quickly subsided into cold numbness that spread to her extremities. Another sudden wave of dizziness brought Alicia slumping to the floor. Quick to follow, Kate sank to her knees beside her, too aggrieved at what her sister was going through to say or do anything more. As Alicia stared blankly at the tiles upon the floor, as if having divulged her very soul from her body, Kate turned towards the doctor, her eyes pleading.

"Are you sure that it checks out? Are you sure you didn't get the wrong results from the test or mixed up her results with someone else's?"

"I checked the results of all the tests myself." The doctor, though more composed now, sounded almost hurt at Kate's implication. "For the pregnancy test, I ran it multiple times to be sure. The test itself hasn't changed in centuries, and it's quite accurate. I don't know how this pregnancy happened, but there was no mistake on my part." He turned towards Alicia, his expression caring, but unapologetic. "I wish with all my heart that this was happier news for you, Ms. Barnes, but I assure you, you are pregnant."

"Doctor, I think you need to give us a moment," Kate said, laying her hand gently on Alicia's exposed back. With a grateful expression, the doctor left the room, leaving the two sisters alone.

Unsure about what else to do, Kate gently rubbed Alicia's back, saying nothing, only letting her sister know that she was there. And Alicia was dead still and silent, her head resting upon her knees like a corpse that in rigor mortis, drawn up upon itself.

"Katie ... I don't understand." Her voice was a low groan, which trembled with stridently repressed sobs. How ..." She swallowed loudly and inhaled a shuddering breath. "What the hell happened? How did this happen? It's not supposed to be able to happen, is it?"

"It shouldn't," Kate said. "But somehow, it happened."

Another long, uncomfortable silence passed between them before Kate decided to speak.

"We could ask the doctor to stop it," she said.

It was as if Alicia woke up from a nightmare. She shook, and her gray eyes flew open, staring hard at Kate, with an anger she had not expected.

"No," she said, almost growling. "In fact, hell no. That isn't an option."

Taken aback by her sudden burst of anger, Kate could only stare blankly. "Um, okay." She swallowed down the sudden wave of embarrassment. "I'm sorry, sis. I didn't know you had such strong feelings about it."

"There's a reason for that," Alicia said, no longer angry. Rather, that anger seemed to transform quickly into distant melancholy. "I thought I'd never have to tell you this, but ... well, mom had it done once."

"Mom? She ..." Kate could hardly believe what she heard. "W ... When? Why?"

"I don't know why, exactly," Alicia said. "I only heard some of the argument between her and dad. I guess dad talked her into doing it. Remember that time that mom was so depressed, and dad had us play away from her for a time? That was what it was. I woke up one night to go to the bathroom and overheard them having it out. She blamed dad for the decision; I don't think she ever forgave herself."

"God..." Kate could not bring any words for this. Their parents were workaholics who used their League science division jobs to cover up their marital problems, but she never knew that their mother had borne this kind of a cross.

"Sorry, Katie," Alicia said. "I thought I'd never have to tell you. But it's because of that night that I promised I'd never do something like that, no matter what."

"I don't blame you, sis," was all that Kate could

say, running her fingers through her sister's hair and touching her forehead to hers. "Damn… I never knew."

"I'm sorry."

"You don't need to be sorry," Kate said. "I just wish I could figure out how this happened to you."

"Knowing you, you're thinking about it right now," Alicia said betraying a tiny, humorless laugh.

Alicia was right. Kate, being an enforcer, had already begun putting her talents to use. Her mind in full detective mode, she thought about the situation carefully, even through this sudden, unexpected, and appalling bit of news. Kate mulled every factor over in her head, and mixed them with all that she had come to learn about Gaeans during her time as an enforcer and as Mukai's friend. It took little time for the pieces to fit together, but once they did, she gasped upon the possible explanation.

At the noise, Alicia looked at her expectantly. A cold sensation passed through Kate's stomach, preventing her from speaking at first. At the sight of her sister's fragile state, she spoke with trepidation, choosing her words with the greatest of care. But she knew that no matter how delicately she presented this hypothesis, Alicia would most likely not take kindly to it.

"Aly, I'm about to give you a hypothesis as to how it could have happened," she said at last, "But I'm pretty sure you won't like it."

"Can't be worse than the news I've endured today," Alicia said, barking out another laugh, just as devoid of humor as the last.

Were that but true, Kate thought, and then swallowed back the apprehensive lump in her throat, steeling herself.

"Okay, here goes … Aly, Kumai is an alpha female. And that means that she will be attracted to beta females and males, not just exclusively one or the other. That's how Gaeans reproduce. Sex for them is, by nature, a three-way thing. Alphas provide an enzyme so that sperm and egg can unite. During sex, they store the sperm from the male in a gland that produces the enzyme, to pass to the female."

"So a male is needed for an alpha to pass sperm on to a beta, so that pregnancy can happen," Alicia said, seeming to stir from her near-comatose state. Her expression was still unreadable. "I do know that much, Katie. Kumai taught me a few things about Gaean birds and bees. So what are you trying to say?"

"Think about it," Kate said.

"To make me pregnant, Kumai would have needed a male?" Alicia said after a moment.

"Yeah." Kate almost whispered it.

"No … no way, sis," Alicia said, the facts coming horribly together in her head. "Kumai would've told me that. She wouldn't have been sleeping around on me! She's not that-"

"Dammit, Aly!" Kate grabbed her sister's shoulders and gave her one stern shake, snapping her back to reality, mid-rant. "Weren't you even listening to what I said? Having two mates is normal for them! As normal as breathing! Alphas seek out both males and betas;

males seek out betas and females, and females seek out alphas and males. You're the 'beta' in this relationship, sis. Kumai must've been with a male somewhere; that's not surprising if you understand Gaeans."

Kate relaxed her hold on her sister, who, to her surprise, did not complain about having been manhandled. Seeing her calmness, she concluded with the one loose piece of information that did not fit in her explanation. "But … for reasons I can't fathom, Kumai didn't tell you."

It was as if a new fire had suddenly been kindled within Alicia's veins. Eyes set firmly, she shot up to her feet and stormed toward her clothes, which hung upon the rack beside the examination table. She nearly tore off the hospital gown and with swift deliberate movements, pulled on underwear, shirt, pants, boots, and her jacket.

"Let's get the hell out of here," she said once she was done. Her tone had become as hard and determined as the look in her eyes. "Pay the doctor, or whatever you have to do to check me out. I'll meet you at the maglev station."

"Wait, what's the rush?" Kate had been only mildly startled at her sister's sudden change. Admittedly, she was grateful in a sense for it, but was also far from relaxed. She hurriedly slung her purse over her shoulder and followed Alicia to the door.

"We're going home, duh!" Alicia did not try to conceal the anger in her voice. "If what you said is true, then Kumai owes me a freaking explanation."

"Wait a sec," Kate said as she followed her sister out the door and into the hallway beyond. She glanced from side to side down the branching sterile white corridors of the League clinic, and by chance, spotted the doctor, not but a few feet away, examining some charts on the I-Link port at his wrist. Leaving Alicia behind, she hurried towards him.

"Doctor," Kate said, drawing the plant-like off-planer's attention. "I know you ran a lot of scans on my sister, but can any of them get a DNA readout?"

"Read … readout …Of the baby, you mean?" The doctor flustered for a second, startled at Kate's sudden appearance and uncertainty at her question. Kate nodded.

"I believe so," the doctor said after a moment's thought. "Why? Do you have any concerns for the baby's health?"

"Take a look at the scans, and call me with the results, okay?" She manipulated the hologram on the doctor's I-Link port and brought it to his notepad. Hurriedly, she scribbled out her phone number and hit the save function. "I want to know if the baby is human or not. Let me know as soon as you get it."

"It won't take long," the doctor said, still bewildered at this sudden change of events. "Aren't you going to wait for the results here?"

"Can't do," Kate said, backing away. "My sister's hell bent on getting back home."

"What for?" The doctor asked. "Why the hurry?"

Kate shrugged, and then pivoted around to catch up

with Alicia. "It's a family thing."

****

Alicia had been walking slowly, and so Kate had had no trouble in catching up. But once at her side, Alicia picked up the pace of her stride. At first, Kate was confused, and then realized that Alicia had only slowed down in order to give her time to catch up.

Alicia had remained silent the entire way, and so Kate did not speak until they boarded the train.

It was early evening, just after rush hour, and the maglevs were mostly empty, as compared to the sardine cans they had become on their way to the League Clinic. Alicia took note of this, and used the opportunity of their privacy to talk.

"You sure this is how it could've been?"

"You mean the explanation of your pregnancy?" Kate asked rhetorically. "Yeah. It's a pretty good chance, unless there's something you're not telling me."

"I never cheated on Kumai," Alicia's voice turned hard, her tone that of warning with just a little bit of danger. "Not during the time she was with me, or when she left."

"I didn't mean to imply anything, sis," Kate tried to be gentle, but her voice had always had a rough edge that kept it just shy of nurturing or sweet. She frowned. "It was a poor choice of words, anyway. I'm sorry. But what about you? Aren't you jumping the gun a bit? I mean, it was just a guess. I don't know for sure what happened, you know. It might not even be Kumai."

"You don't believe that, and you know it," Alicia shook her head. "We've only been reacquainted for around a year, but I know you, Katie. You haven't changed much from when we were kids. You're still as sharp as a tack. You've gotta be in order to be to be an enforcer. You're a detective. You get things! Facts come together neat and tidy for you, and I'll bet credits to krid that you're right."

A shrill, electronic ringing from Kate's I-Link port interrupted the conversation. Kate paused and switched the device to its phone setting.

The doctor's familiar tree-like face popped up in the hologram, rippling for a moment at first, until the image, a static photo, solidified.

"Doctor," Kate said attentively. Did you find out what I asked?

Recognizing the doctor's face, Alicia lunged forward. "Found out what?"

"Yes, I did," the doctor said, his voice piped directly into Kate's eardrum via the INplant at her temple. Kate glanced at Alicia and gestured for her to wait.

"Like hell, I'll wait!" Alicia said, incensed. "What did you ask him?"

"The baby is Gaean …" the doctor said, his voice coming in over Alicia's protest, "… well, two-thirds Gaean, as it would appear. The rest of her code is human."

"Her?" Kate said with mild surprise.

"Yes. It's a girl," the Doctor answered. "Not an

alpha, but a true female."

"Thanks, doc. You were a big help," Kate said, and hung up before any more questions could be asked.

"What the hell did you ask him?" Alicia said, her voice shrill with apprehensive anger.

"Relax, Aly." Kate shut off her I-Link port and leaned back in her seat. "I just asked about the baby's race. He let me know that it's two-thirds Gaean. I wanted to see if Kumai had been with a human, or with one of her own kind."

"And … it's a girl?" Alicia asked, her voice quieter.

"That's what the doctor said."

"A girl …" was all that Alicia could say as her anger diffused. "Well, I guess what you said about Kumai does make sense." She stiffened suddenly. "Wait, what? Hold on; rewind there, sis. Did you just say 'two thirds'?"

"Alphas take two mates, remember?"

"Yeah, but I didn't know that alphas actually contributed to the baby's genes. I thought that it was just an enzyme they gave."

"Oh, that," Kate said. "Well, they do do that, but they also contribute some DNA to the mix. That same gland that produces the enzyme and stores sperm cells also produces something like a virus."

"A *virus*?" Instinctively, Alicia grabbed at her abdomen, her eyes wide in sudden horror.

"It's completely harmless; don't worry." Kate drawled out her words soothingly. "And it only targets sex cells anyway. It replaces small portions of DNA in sperm and egg cells with DNA from the alpha female."

"Oh." Feeling better, but just a little bit stupid, Alicia relaxed in her seat as her sister had done. "You know a lot about Gaeans, Katie."

"Helps to have a friend who is a Gaean," Kate said with a playful grin. "And the I-Link is for more than just porn and vids of people hurting themselves."

"So you really think that Kumai was with another Gaean?" Alicia asked.

"Seems that way," Kate replied, "unless you know any other way."

"I'd still prefer to hear it out of her own mouth."

A few silent moments later, a thought occurred to Alicia.

"You know, I'll bet that it had something to do with what she was so evasive about."

"Evasive? Kumai?" Kate turned lazily toward her sister. "What do you mean?"

"The night she came back, I asked her where she'd been for the last five months, and what she'd been doing. And she kept giving me these short, one-word answers. Then she fed me some line about how it was a difficult time for her, and how she didn't want to talk about it at the time. She said she'd tell me later, but later never came. Hell, I'd all but forgotten about it until just now."

"Well, that *does* seem interesting," Kate said, her mind slipping back into detective mode. "You said she gave you short, one-word answers. Do you remember what they were?"

"Yeah, I think so." It took Alicia a moment to recall, but the memories soon resurfaced. "She only said two things: that she'd gone back home, and that she had been teaching. That's pretty much it."

"Home… teaching…" Kate mulled these words over in her head, attempting to try and fit them into her hypothesis, but try as she might, she could not seem to make the connection. The only scenario that even halfway fit would be a tryst between Kumai and a male student, but teaching on Gaea was a very sacred institution, so much so that all teachers were chemically neutered and then sequestered in their schools during their tenure in order to devote themselves fully to academia, rather than carnal desires. And the random checks for faithfulness in their dosages were very strict. Teachers who were found to have skipped on their doses were punished severely: kept under house arrest without pay until their tenures were completed. And tenures ran four years, at the minimum. There was no way that Kumai would have been able to get back home after only three months.

"Unless she escaped…?" The words fell quietly from Kate's mouth.

"Unless who escaped?" Alicia's question made Kate realize that she had spoken that last thought aloud. "And from where?"

"Oh, I just came up with another scenario," Kate said, and then explained her recent musings.

"Yeah, that does sound like a little bit of a stretch," Alicia admitted after Kate had finished. "Wow. They really do that to teachers? Neuter them and sequester them in schools?"

"It's their way." Kate gave a lazy "what-can-you-do" shrug. "But they don't sequester them for life."

"Yeah, I know; you told me," Alicia said. "Kumai's been teaching me a lot of stuff, but I guess I still have a lot to learn." A look of mixed sadness and frustration came to her face. "I just wish I knew how this happened."

The computerized voice of the maglev's autoconductor announced their stop. Kate stood with Alicia and walked out onto the platform.

"You'll find out soon enough, I think." She reached out and touched her sister's shoulder with a reassuring smile. "I wish I knew what you were going through. But you're my sister, and I'm here for you, okay?"

Alicia, swallowing back the emotions that had already been building within her during the trip, smiled, and pulled Kate into a quick embrace.

"I know, sis. And I can't thank you enough."

****

"Look, Aly, just don't bite Kumai's head off."

"No promises on that," Alicia's tone was flat and utterly serious as she punched in the code on the front door's lock. A shrill three-tone series of beeps preceded the sound of the door unlocking, and Alicia turned the knob. She began to step through into the foyer, but paused as she noticed in her peripheral vision that Kate had not followed.

"What's wrong?" She asked turning back towards her sister.

"Oh, you wanted me to come with you?" Kate glanced furtively back towards her motorcycle, parked just outside the gate.

"Why wouldn't I?" Alicia said, fixing Kate with a puzzled look.

"I guess I just thought that this would be something you'd want to discuss with Kumai in private."

"Actually, I think I want you here for this," Alicia said after a moment's thought. "I'm already having a sucky day, and I kinda have a feeling that this won't be easy. I might need a mediator."

"It might be easier than you think," Kate said. "Kumai's very easy to talk to."

"I'm not worried about that, sis; I'm worried about what she'll tell me."

Alicia stepped over the threshold and into the house as Kate followed. No sooner had she entered than she started calling for Kumai in Glossiu.

"She's in the den," Kate said, noticing Kumai's appearance at the foot of the staircase when Alicia passed by the den's entrance.

"Kumai is here, tir-Alicia."

Alicia froze in the hallway and then backtracked, meeting Kate and peering into the den where Kumai sat down on the tan-colored suede sofa to wait for her.

"Your Glossiu is improving," Kumai said with an approving smile, "but the way you called for Kumai has more intimate connotations that you did not intend." She smiled, but her expression vanished once she noticed that Alicia did not return it. Taking a less relaxed posture, she gazed quizzically at Alicia as she sat beside her. Kate took a seat in the couch across from the sofa and love seat.

One look at the off-planer brought to Kate's mind the conversation between Alicia and Mukai that she had walked in on at the restaurant. Kumai's clothes were indeed fitting quite a bit tighter around her previously near-nonexistent chest. If her clothes were not already uncomfortable for her, she surmised that they soon would be.

Alicia fidgeted for a moment, not a sound escaping from her mouth, but the desire to speak strong in her eyes as she glanced at Kumai. The off-planer's liquid black eyes were unreadable, as always.

"You look terrible, tir-Alicia," Kumai said, trying to pry words from her mate's mouth. "What is wrong?"

Alicia closed her eyes and heaved a very audible sigh.

"I'm pregnant."

Kumai's mouth fell open, forming into a soundless "Oh." For the first time, emotion was present in her black eyes. It was impossible to miss, as they had widened into twice their normal size. Not a breath came from Kumai as she stiffened and then sat motionless and stone silent.

"We went to the doctor to make sure," Alicia continued without prompting. Her voice had become breathy, almost frantic. "I knew something was wrong.

I've been weak, sick, dizzy; I didn't even realize that I missed my last period until today. I should've suspected it, but I didn't want to believe it. And now…"

Her speech slowed down, and her voice strained into a broken sob. "…and now…"

Quickly, Kumai reached out and pulled Alicia to her breast, her fingers pressing into the back of her head. Alicia, her face pressed to the off-planer's growing bosom, wept openly and loudly, her cries muffled by the fabric of clothes. Automatically, Alicia's arms wrapped around Kumai's slender waist, the tears saturating the cloth of the lapels on the expensive-looking business suit. Silently, Kumai held on to Alicia, allowing her to cry all that she could, melting away all the emotions that had spilled over. She comforted her with soft words in her dialect, which Kate, who had watched on silently, only barely knew. In time, Alicia's sobs softened, and her head moved, freeing her mouth to speak without obstruction.

"How?" She asked, her words coming out in a shuddering whisper. "How did it happen?"

"Kumai expected you would find out soon," Kumai said, running her long, slender fingers through Alicia's silken ebony mop. "But Kumai did not expect this to happen. Kumai did not even think it was possible, until the change began."

"Change…?" Alicia lifted her head, revealing bloodshot eyes that gazed intensely at her mate.

Kumai made only the vaguest of nods. "The change … in Kumai." The off-planer's hand moved from

Alicia's hair, and rested indicatively upon her more ample chest. "In *kalampra*, this is a sign of a successful mating."

The connection was like a lightning bolt in Kate's mind. So that was what Mukai had been going on about! It must have been how she was able to suspect pregnancy after listening to Alicia's complaints. At this realization, Kate spoke up for the first time.

"You mean that when your mate is pregnant, you begin to… grow?"

"Yes. It is the only time such a change will happen. Our bodies … taste our *kalampu* mate, and when they are with child, the body reacts to prepare."

That was right; Gaeans were not all that different from humans, and alpha females could breastfeed their young as well. Kate could have kicked herself over having forgotten about that detail.

"But *how* did it happen?" Alicia's voice stretched to where it was nearly a squeal. "You had to have been with a male, right? Is that what you couldn't tell me? Was that why you went back to Gaea?"

"Not originally," Kumai answered. Sadness and guilt were now evident upon her face, despite her unreadable eyes, from which tears now flowed. "You must understand, tir-Alicia, times are difficult back home. The economy is …" She frowned, and she searched the air for the right words. At last, defeated, she used Glossiu, "*zan-ka-zat.*"

Alicia, having shut off her translation matrix, made a puzzled face at the unfamiliar word.

"'In recession,'" Kate said.

Kumai smiled thankfully. "Kumai could not return to Kumai's original job. Tisvard was the business where Kumai worked before Kumai met you. But when Kumai tried to return, there were no more openings. Kumai searched for weeks, and then finally was accepted as a *shappaiyah*."

"You said you were a teacher," Alicia said, sounding almost hurt. "Why did you lie to me?"

Kumai appeared stricken at Alicia's accusation, her mouth open, but wordless. Kate, quick to understand, spoke in her stead, explaining. "A *shappaiyah* is a teacher, Aly."

Alicia shook her head. "But I thought you said that they-"

"A *shappaiyah* is different," Kate said, again wincing inwardly over her previous failure in logic. "I'm sorry; I should've remembered this. A *shappaiyah* is ... well, a Gaean 'sex ed' teacher. Only they don't just teach it from textbooks. They're hands-on."

Alicia stared blankly for a moment, her expression unreadable until a quiet "oh" escaped her lips. "That's ... weird."

"Sis, some races don't have the same kinds of hang-ups about sex as we do," Kate said in rebuke.

"It is quite common on Gaea," Kumai said, "not 'weird' at all. Sex is a complex thing among us, and when we are of age, *shappaiyah* teach us to do it properly and safely."

"Kumai chose to teach *kelempra* only," Kumai

explained. "Kumai had found you, and Kumai hoped that one would call to Kumai, and the pain of leaving you would be eased."

"Okay, so you didn't lie to me," Alicia said, sounding no less hurt. "But why did you keep this from me?"

"Kumai has learned of humans." Kumai turned her head away and a slight blush came to the blue of her face, tinting it faintly violet. "Kumai knows that relationships can be a sensitive thing among humans, easily misunderstood. Kumai knew that telling you everything might have made you upset. Kumai was afraid."

"Oh, blueberry…" Alicia frowned, but there was no accusation in her eyes, only mild disappointment, but restrained by sympathy. Still, Kumai bit her lip and averted her gaze, or so it seemed. Her expression had come as close to shame as any human's.

"Kumai also believed that becoming with child by a Gaean was impossible for humans, so Kumai neglected *kolis…*" She quickly explained once she saw the confused look in Alicia's eyes. "… purification."

It was only when Alicia asked what "purification" meant that Kate had to explain, as Kumai seemed to have a hard time putting it in words. "It's a ritual that alpha female *shappaiyah* normally go through after they leave the service," she said. "Remember what I told you about that gland they have? After they're done with this 'teaching,' to ensure that any children they make with their mates are their own, they have to basically purge the gland."

Kumai gave Kate a grateful look as Alicia digested what was said. It took a moment before understanding dawned upon her.

"I'm guessing you didn't … purge," she said to Kumai.

"If Kumai had known, Kumai would have," Kumai's expression was one of deep pain as her fingers curled around Alicia's arms. She spoke in a soft, brittle voice. "Kumai never meant for this to happen, tir-Alicia. Kumai thought that there was no risk. Never was there a child born between our people. Kumai is so, so sorry!"

Alicia wanted to be angry. Kumai had basically dropped the ball on her people's version of "safe sex" and now Alicia had to pay the price. She wanted that anger so badly; it was a desperate longing that maddeningly failed to reach the surface.

Alicia squeezed her eyes shut, her body trembling with impotent frustration at the deluge of emotion that would not come. Only tears came in abundance. They flowed freely as she grasped Kumai's sleeves.

"Dammit, blueberry… Why can't I be angry with you?" She growled through bared teeth.

"Because you know that there's no need to be angry with her," Kate said. "She didn't know that you could get pregnant by a Gaean. Hell, I didn't know it either. You have plenty of humans who hook up with off-planers, and a few do produce kids, but it's just never been studied with Gaeans. Can you blame Kumai for not knowing?"

Alicia scowled at first. Then she brought her eyes to Kumai's. This lasted only a second as she saw for the first time, a glimmer of emotion in them. And this emotion was pain. Poor Kumai, who had never hurt her in any way, felt as guilty about this as anyone would. And of course, this child was, in part, hers. Ashamed at her desire to be angry, she hung her head, turning away from both her sister and her mate.

"I'm…sorry, tir-Kumai," she whispered, switching to Glossiu. "I know you didn't mean this." She shuddered, and then slipped back into English. "It's just that … well, damn … I'm not ready to be a mom!"

"Kumai does not feel ready to be *issa* either," Kumai said.

"*Issa* …?"

"Glossiu word for what Kumai will be to the child." Kumai smiled as if for the first time today. "*Lamsa* is 'mother,' which is what you will be. *Lemsa* is 'father.'"

"You …" Alicia interrupted her sentence with a loud, wet sniffle. "You're saying you … want it? The baby?"

"Kumai is shocked by the circumstances …" Kumai nodded, and her fingers went to Alicia's face. She brushed back her hair and caressed her pale cheek with her fingers, bringing a blush to the skin. Alicia, in turn, grasped Kumai's hand in her own and pressed it against her cheek as tears flowed. "But yes. Kumai will be *issa*."

"Then if you want it, I want it too," she said. "I will be *lamsa*."

Kumai's smile widened, and Alicia reflected the expression. "*Mel'idii*, tir-Alicia."

Alicia allowed Kumai's hand to guide her face closer to her mate. "*Mel'idii*," she whispered.

Alicia looked up after the kiss had ended to see that Kate was nowhere to be found. She looked at the clock and, noting how much time had passed, laughed self-effacingly. "Damn. It looks like Katie took off. I didn't even hear her get up or hear the door shut."

"Kumai did not either," Kumai said with a titter of her own.

"Melody!" Alicia suddenly breathed excitedly.

"*Mel'idii*, tir-Alicia," Kumai said, now laughing at her mate's excitement.

"No, no. I mean 'Melody.' That would be a good name for her."

"It is *kalampu*?" Kumai said with pleasant surprise.

Alicia nodded. "Yeah. A girl. *Our* girl. Does the name sound weird? I mean I know that it sounds like 'I love you' in your language. Would that be strange to Gaeans?"

"No ..." Kumai whispered, "not strange at all, tir-Alicia." Tenderly, she touched her forehead to Alicia's. Her smile was radiant and strikingly white against her blue skin. "It is beautiful. More beautiful than any name among Kumai's people. Kumai likes the name."

"Melody," Alicia said, enunciating as if tasting the name.

"Our Melody," Kumai said, as her hand went gently

to Alicia's abdomen. Alicia placed her hand atop Kumai's.

"I guess that means we'll have to cut the tour short," Alicia said. And Kumai laughed.

THE END

ABOUT THE AUTHOR

I am a native of Louisiana and current resident of Lafayette. An avid and frequent reader of science fiction and fantasy, I began writing in the eleventh grade. I am a graduate of McNeese State University in Lake Charles. I am a 'classic nerd' and prolific writer who has had dreams of authorship since childhood. I sketch perhaps even more prolifically than I write, and have drawings of just about every character my warped imagination has come up with. I hope to continue sharing these ideas, characters, and stories with others for years to come.